YA Books by
Lucas & Sophia McWilliams
Hunters of Eternal Lies

YA Books by
Lucas McWilliams
Savage Summer
Eternal Hunt

**Middle age Books by father-daughter
team Lucas and Sophia McWilliams**

Wielders #1 The Journey Begins
Wielders #2 First Battle
Wielders #3 The Hunter
Wielders #4 Silver Town Championship
Wielders #5 Lost Friend
Wielders #6 Secretes in the Dark
Wielders #7 Water Temple
Wielders #8 Returning Home
And look for more coming out soon!

www.Wielders.us
www.LucasMcWilliams.com

Hunters of Eternal Lies, The Becket Chronicles
By
Lucas & Sophia McWilliams

ISBN# 978-1-939037-20-6

www.Wielders.us
www.LucasMcWilliams.com

Published 2016 by Coval Press

For my wife and three wonderful girls who bring a smile to my lips each day. I love you more than anything.

Special thanks to the dedicated few that really went above and beyond in helping me complete this process. Joan, Larry, Kay, Marissa, Skye, Genevieve & Lucas's lovely wife Laura.

And thank you, dear reader!

Table of Contents

Hunters of Eternal Lies
The Becket Chronicles
By Lucas & Sophia McWilliams

Chapter One:
The Old Country

Everything that happened in Texas makes me reflect on my life. I used to be able to touch an object and know emotions and visions associated with that object. However, something happened to me several years ago and I lost my gift.

I was born Rebecca Nicola Shaw. My mother's maiden name is Degano, which is a big name back in the old country. For my mother's family, the old country is Italy but not the touristy Italy. It is not Rome or Venice. It is way out in the mountains up north. To hear my Grandmother tell it, the Degano family has always lived in Carnia, Italy, in the foothills of the Alps.

Seven valleys form Carnia. Each of the valleys has a stream running through it from which the valleys take their name. My family is from Degano Valley or Val Degano in Italian. My family shares the name of the river, thus the name of the valley. It is a sparse, rugged place in the lower Alps.

My mother spoke to me and my siblings in the old languages of her homeland and we visited Italy twice each year. We visited the old country once over Christmas and for three months in the summer. Needless to say, I picked up the languages, and yes, there were more than one. English was our native tongue, my father and all our friends in America spoke only English, but mother would not talk to us at all unless we used one of the dialects of Carnia, which included Italian first, then Friulian, which is the region Carnia is in, then Slovene and German because many of her old friends spoke them, and we had some Slovenia and German friends. It was a pain growing up speaking different languages, but if you wanted to have dinner or do anything fun, you had to ask in one of my mother's native tongues.

On top of all those languages, I was raised Catholic and went to Catholic schools. My mother insisted that I take Latin every year it was offered, so I learned to read and write Latin quite well.

When we went home, we always stayed at my Grandmother Degano's house. She had a beautiful place next to a mountain spring that created a nice little stream to play in. Some of the water was piped into the house and supplied the running water. It was pretty rustic at grandmother's. She had a generator that ran some lights and for extra heat in the winter. Most of the time, grandmother would just use oil lamps or candles and not mess with the generator. My uncle lived next to grandmother and took care of anything she needed done. One of my uncle's sons worked grandmother's fields and tended her flock of sheep. Grandmother would shear the sheep with me every summer right after I arrived and we would spend the summer spinning the wool into yarn. Every Christmas grandmother would knit me something from some of the wool we made over the summer. I loved my grandmother and that valley.

My mother always talked of grandmother having the gift or the sight. She could see things others could not. I have even heard that she could give someone the evil eye and bad luck or death would come to them. I never believed about the evil eye, but I did believe in the sight, because I saw it work and I possessed it from birth. Gran and I would practice my skills whenever I was with her. I also could naturally tell when something bad was going to happen to me or a person I cared deeply for. I even grew to where I could see glimpses of the coming danger and learn how to avoid or prevent it. Sometimes the danger could not be avoided, but most of the time it could. Gran did not have this ability, but she knew about it in the old stories of our family. Her mother had had the danger sense, as I called it.

I also had the ability to touch objects and receive glimpses of important events in their existence. I could tune into the emotions that were left on an item from people who previously possessed it. It was a wonderful skill that Gran also possessed. She created games for me to practice my skill, showing me an object, asking me to figure out the item's history and who had possessed it. Each summer, Gran had a new box of items she had collected to practice on.

My mother knew of my gifts, but their existence was kept from my father. My father was an American and did not believe in the sight. He came with my mother to Degano Valley every few years but never stayed too long. The old world Degano family was not very accepting of my mother's choice of a husband. They were also not happy that we lived so far away. They were simple people, most of whom had never traveled more than fifty miles from their homes their whole lives. It was a much different world from living in a huge city like Seattle. I do not think my father minded not being welcome at Gran's house. It gave him a reason to get back to work. My father was an executive, a high-level manager of marketing for one of the up and coming software companies in Seattle. He seemed to like his job and traveled a lot. He made good money and came from way better money, so I was allowed to buy anything I wanted.

 8

When I was sixteen, we spent the summer at Gran's like normal. I did miss my cell and the internet, but I liked being with Gran. There was a big party scheduled for me on the summer solstice. It was to celebrate my coming of age. This meant I was of marriageable age, at least that is what my mother and Gran thought. I did not want to get married. All the eligible men were invited to dinner one by one before the day of the party so I could get to know them. I think I met every man from the age of sixteen through thirty who lived in a fifty-mile radius. I did like a few, but I was not looking for a husband and wanted to go to college. College was a dirty word in my Gran's house. She loved me and wanted me to have a family and a happy life in her valley as she did. I could tell that she never forgave my mother for leaving and not raising her children close by. I humored my Gran as my mother did. I think my mother would have been happy to let me marry and stay there the rest of my life, but she also supported me going to college, just not in front of Gran.

When it was almost the summer solstice and my coming of age party, a man came by after dinner for drinks. Gran spoke of him as a great man, confiding that I was honored by him even taking the time to come see me. I was to be on my best behavior while he was at the house. I am pretty sure he was from Slovenia but spoke perfect Friulian while at Gran's house. He walked with a cane that had a lifelike silver bat head handle. He did not seem to have a limp or need the cane in any way, it was more like a prop or symbol of power. He tapped it on the ground as he walked. I remember hearing it before he came to the door. The tap, tap, tapping of his cane on the stone walk came to my ears in rhythm with the beating of my heart. I looked out to see him but found it odd that I saw no car, carriage or horse. We lived miles from the nearest house except for my uncle's home. The man with the cane had not come from that direction.

I opened the door. He stood in the doorway and stared into me as I moved out of the way for him to enter. I wondered why he did not come on in the house.

"Are you going to invite me in?" the man with the cane challenged, softly but powerfully. He was obviously someone who expected to give orders and be obeyed.

"Please do come in, I am Becket," I sputtered, stepping back to let him in the room.

The gentleman bowed to me and introduced himself before walking across the threshold into Gran's house. "I am Antal Degano. I am pleased to finally meet you, Becket," he commented, walking past me into the house.

Antal Degano was around six feet tall and mysteriously handsome. He was younger than I thought he would be since my Gran thought of him so

highly. I guessed his age to be mid-to-early twenties. He had dark hair that was cut short. His face was clean-shaven and a little pale for summer. He had strong cheekbones that defined his V shaped face. His chin was narrow but pleasing to the eye when put with the rest of his features. His eyes were what really drew me in. He had dark eyes with bright amber flecks that almost sparkled when they caught the light.

Tonight Gran turned off the generator and we only used candles. I thought it a strange thing to do but she insisted.

We all sat together on the good soft back chairs Gran reserves for guests. Almost immediately, Gran has a chore for she and my mother in the kitchen. They excused themselves, leaving me alone with Antal. Gran has never done this before so I was alert. She was always sure to chaperone whenever men called.

"Your birth name is Rebecca, is that correct?" Antal inquired, looking at me.

"Yes, but one of my friends started calling me Becket in grade school and it just stuck. I like Becket. It is very unusual and I run into so many other girls named Rebecca in school," I explained.

"I like Becket as well. I think it suits you. You are not the average girl, so an unusual name fits. Do you want to stay here in Degano Valley or return to America?" Antal questioned, watching me.

"I want to go to college and see where that takes me. I love Degano Valley but the world is a big place and I want to experience it," I answered, wondering what Antal is getting at.

"Your grandmother has told me you have the abilities of her mother as well as her own gifts. Is this true?" Antal asked.

"Umm. Grandmother does not like me to talk about those kinds of things," I hesitated and wondered why he knew so much about me.

"I understand your caution, you do not know me yet. I trust what your grandmother has already told me. What do you plan to do with your gifts?" Antal probed, taking a sip of his drink and setting the glass back on the side table with a soft clink.

"I have never really thought about it. You mean, like a job?" I reply.

"They could be useful in various employments, but they are a great gift to not be squandered away. You should use them for a purpose. This is something I could help you with," Antal suggested, still watching me.

"I am still young. I am sure I will figure it out. I mainly use my abilities when I am here with Gran to learn things about people," I insist.

"That is good. Those experiences will serve you well. Would you stay in our valley if you had a purpose? What if you could also travel but you called Degano Valley home? Would you stay then?"

He was making me uncomfortable and I answered a little sharply. "I don't know. I would need to know more about this goal. More about what you are asking," I admitted wondering if he thinks he can be my special purpose. I wonder if he wants me to marry him.

"Think about what I have said. Excuse me for a moment." Antal says as he leaves the room and goes in the kitchen to join Gran and my mother.

I hear my mother yelling and wonder what is going on. I look at Antal's empty chair and see his cane propped up against it. I look to make sure no one is around. Then I get up and walk over to the cane to get a closer look. I pick it up and immediately see a vision of blood. I see blood everywhere in the room covering me. I fall to the floor and the blood rises to cover me until there is only darkness.

****

I wake up in a hospital bed with my father beside me. He did not come to the valley this year so I wonder where he came from.

"Becket! Are you all right, baby girl?" My dad exclaims, leaning over and hugging me so tight, I can hardly breathe.

"Uh," is all I can get out as I start to choke.

There are tubes down my throat and in my arms. What is going on? Nurses swarm into the room and push my dad away. A long time passes with them taking out the tubes in my throat and rest of my body.

I overhear that I was in a coma for a month. What happened to me?

When they are done with me, I talk to my dad. My mouth is dry and feels bad. I am hungry but my throat hurts. I am not a happy camper. The last thing I remember is touching Antal's cane, but it is fuzzy after that.

My father explains to me that I have been in a coma for a month. I was staying at my Grans but they could not get me to eat so I was brought to the hospital. My mom and Gran did not tell my dad anything had happened to me for almost three weeks. He came as soon as he heard about my condition and has been here ever since. He was first told I fell and hit my head when my mother called him on the phone. Later in person, my mother tried to explain about my gift and me falling into a vision and that I was fighting to come back from it. My dad was angry, confused, tired, and much relieved I was awake from the coma.

I knew I missed my coming of age party. All I could remember was touching Antal's cane and being drowned in blood. I had nightmares every night, sometimes several times about being drowned in blood. I wasn't getting much sleep but was getting my strength back.

Summer vacation was almost over and my dad wanted to take me home. I heard my parents arguing about whether to go home or not. In the end, my father won and we left for Seattle without saying goodbye to Gran. I wanted to see Gran but was glad to be going home. I know I did not want to see Antal or his cane again.

The nightmares continued, but slowly became less frequent. I found I could no longer sense things from objects. I still had my danger sense, and if anything, it was more acute. I missed being able to read the emotional imprint on an object, and looked forward to asking Gran about it next time we went to see her.

The thing was, we did not go back to Degano Valley. I know this caused many arguments but my father put his foot down. I guess I almost died last time I was at Gran's and my father had heard enough about my gift. Christmas came and went without a trip to Gran's. Then summer with no trip to Gran's. I missed Gran but fell into a routine of not going.

I did rebel a little but I was a teenager. I started really getting into extreme sports. My gift of danger sense gave me an edge that let me push the limit of stupid stunts all the time. I already knew how to snow ski, snowboard, mountain bike and do gymnastics. I pushed all those activities to the limit and learned more. I got into motorcycle racing, mountain climbing and martial arts. I did not go too far down the path of rebellion to lose sight of college, but enough to freak out my parents.

I went to Berkeley and got a degree in marketing because my dad liked it. I was always personable and well liked. I landed a job at a music mag in Seattle after graduation and everything seemed on track. That was until a month ago when I went for a vacation to the Goodrest Ranch. That was it's own horror story. The only thing good to come out of that vacation so far is that I got my gift back. I can read emotional impressions on objects again.

Chapter Two:
Goodrest

Everything has changed because of what happened in Texas, so I relive the experience to hopefully learn some new insight into what really happened.

My eyes flicker open as the hair on the back of my neck stands straight up. I was asleep with my head against the window of this old rickety bus until I sensed danger. I sit up straight just in time to avoid my head slamming into the window by the jolt to the bus from a large pothole.

"Ahhh," a couple of people scream on the bus.

"Damn it, Steve, watch where you're going!" I yell at the driver, grabbing the back of the seat in front to steady myself.

I have been on some bumpy roads in my life but this one may be the worst. I think Steve intentionally drives into every pothole and rut he can find. I can't believe this junky bus doesn't even have air conditioning. I feel like a school kid riding on some crazy hot field trip.

When are we going to get there? We have been driving for three hours and twenty minutes already. I hope this dude ranch is worth it. I just wanted to take a week off and learn to ride a horse, not rupture a disk from a bus ride.

The small bus is only about half way full. There is Steve, the prick of a cowboy driving us. He was just a real charmer to everyone. He was in a hurry and pushed everyone to get "a move on." He practically threw our luggage into the back of the bus. The worst thing was that sick looking lump in his lip. I knew what the bulge was when I saw him spit right in the middle of a sentence while he was talking to Mr. Wilson. I can't stand men who chew tobacco. Once in college, I kissed a guy at a party who was chewing and swallowed some of that black vile juice. Yuck! I spit the juice all over him and ran off to wash my mouth out. Never again for this girl.

In the front of the bus is Mr. John Johnson, another ranch guest. John is here to try to spend some father-son time with his jock son, Jim. John Johnson is an accountant in Dallas. Jim Johnson is seventeen, so, of course he, thinks he knows everything. Jim has already told anyone who will listen that he is the quarterback on his high school football team. He must have been hit a few times too many in the head because it is freaking hot and no one else is wearing a jacket, let alone a thick wool letterman's coat. I bet he thinks it will impress the ladies. I saw the way he watched me when I climbed on the bus. I could tell he was imagining me naked, typical horny teenage boy dreams.

Sue and Rachel sit in the seat in front of me. Rachel is a registered nurse at a small clinic and Sue is a

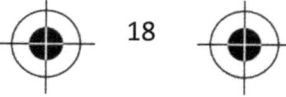

model and dancer. I get the feeling that Sue mostly dances with a pole, if you know what I mean. They are both very attractive women but older than I am by at least five years. They are together, like in the biblical way. I thought Jim was going to explode and drool all over himself when they started making out to pass the time.

Next, we have the lovely Wilson family, on their second honeymoon. Tina Wilson does seem like a genuinely nice lady. She is around my age and teaches first grade. Her husband Tim is more outgoing. I knew he was in sales after hearing him talk for just a few minutes. He is a Timeshare sales representative, and to hear him talk, a damn good one. The Wilsons are here to see if the Goodrest Ranch could work as a timeshare. Guess it is kind of a working vacation. Tina tells me they get to go on trips like this several times a year for Tim's job.

Then, finally, on the bus is me, Rebecca Nicola Shaw, but everyone calls me Becket. My mother would want me to remember that her family name is Degano, a noble name from the old country. I'm five feet seven and a quarter inches tall but I tell everyone I'm five eight. I have a toned athletic build and am blessed with an ample bust line. I often have the whole bad girl thing going but I am not that bad. I play hard and party hard but am not into doing things that will land me in jail. I like to play extreme sports. I have toned it down in the last couple of months since I graduated from Berkeley with a marketing degree. I just landed a job working at a small Seattle music magazine and am pretty psyched.

Currently my hair is black and short. My hairstyles change all the time but are never too conservative and always sexy.

We all chat on the long bus trip and get to know each other. Jim is either playing his handheld, listening to his Mp3 while trying to sleep or undressing the females with his eyes. He does not really talk much and if he did talk, I bet he would not have much to say. His dad, John, has a laptop and seems to be doing work most of the bus ride.

The other five of us get acquainted and click pretty well. I figure I will be hanging out with this group for the week on the Goodrest Ranch. Tim is a pretty funny guy once you get past the "I'm gonna sell you something phase" of meeting him. I like his wife, Tina, from the start. I think we can actually be friends. Rachel is more genuine than Sue is. I guess working with sick people all the time gives you a compassionate heart. Sue is a little full of herself and wants to be the alpha female in the group. I also see the way she looks at me when Rachel is not watching and I do not like where that is going, although it is better than Jim ogling me.

It is nearly dusk when we finally make it to the ranch. I must say it is a pretty place, especially with the beginnings of a nice sunset framing it. The ranch is nestled down in a valley with a good size stream running through it. The main house is three stories and looks to have a basement. It sits just a stone's throw from the stream. I can see it has a great big deck all the way around and a nice looking hot tub on the backside facing the stream. There is a very large stable for horses with a loft for hay. There are also a couple of smaller out buildings and corrals with some horses in them. There is a carport area with mostly tractors parked under it.

As we pull up, a man and woman come out. I expect they are the Tolesons, the family who runs the ranch. I see another man come out of the barn and a third working over by the corral. The one by the corral is young and yummy. I may have to let him teach me how to ride, even though I already know that kind of riding.

We all pile out of the bus and I am surprised when no one throws themselves on the ground and kisses it, thanking the Lord that damn bumpy hot ride is over. The Tolesons' come over and introduce themselves. "Howdy y'all. Welcome to the Goodrest Ranch! We're sure glad you'uns could make it down to our neck of the woods. I am Keith Toleson and this purty little thang is Anny. She's got supper almost ready. Get your things and we'll show you to your rooms. Then get washed up fer supper," Mr. Toleson says, waving us all into the house.

The ever-helpful Steve throws our bags at us as we come to the back of the bus. He manages to hand Tim and Jim their bags all nice like and I can tell he rides sidesaddle. We walk in the house and the first room is a huge living room/dining room combo that takes up half the downstairs. There is also a big fireplace to sit around on cold nights. It is very rustic with large wood furniture and the stuffed heads of animals around on the walls. There is the obligatory trophy fish and some western paintings. It is nice and fun but I would have gone in a different direction, but then, I would never live out here in the middle of nowhere Texas.

The rest of the downstairs is dedicated to the Toleson's living area and kitchen. It is all out of sight from the guest area. The second floor is primarily for men. It has six rooms and a shared bath. We are the only guests right now. Mr. Johnson and his son Jim stay on the second floor. There are so many free rooms that they decide to each take a room to themselves. The third floor also has six bedrooms and a shared bathroom and is usually the girl's floor. The Wilson's are given a choice of which floor to stay on since they are man and wife. Tim chooses to be on the third floor with us girls. Rachel and Sue share a room at the end of the hall furthest from the bathroom. I take the room across the hall from them. The Wilsons take the room one over from mine on the same side of the hall. This puts them cattycorner from the bathroom but not sharing a wall with it. There are stairs at both ends of the hall that go all the way down to ground floor.

Most of the rooms have two single beds in them. The Wilsons get a room with a queen size bed. Rachel and Sue have to push their singles together. I do the same in my room as I am used to a bigger bed. We get just a little settled and the dinner bell rings. It's an iron triangle, like the one you see used in old western movies. We all make our way downstairs and sit at one huge oak table.

Mrs. Toleson has the table well prepared and most of the food is already on it when I arrive. We all sit down and sip our sweet tea waiting for the last of the guests to arrive. The Tolesons sit with us and we have a nice dinner full of good southern home cooking. Rachel is a vegetarian and Sue is giving her crap about it as she eats her steak.

After dinner, we sit in the living room and enjoy each other's company. Someone mentions the hot tub and most of us go to change for it. It is around ten o'clock and I am kind of hoping Jim will turn in but I do not count on it. I get back downstairs and out to the tub with the girls in tow. We three get in and have the hot tub all to ourselves for a while. We chat about where we live and what we do. Sue talks the most and definitely likes to hear the sound of her own voice. She is bending over showing me her latest tattoo that descends below her bikini line when Jim walks up. He stops in his tracks and stares at Sue's butt. Sue could give a damn about Jim. She pulls her bottoms down even further, giving her ass a little shake. The tattoo is of a dragon that starts at her crack and goes up her back several inches. The dragon's wings are to either side, one on each butt cheek. I have just never been into the whole tramp stamp on your lower back mentality. Someday Sue's butt will sag and no one will want to look at that faded tattoo.

We look over at Jim and it's obvious by the bulge in his pants that he would like to fly on Sue's dragon. He looks down, puts both hands over his full pants and runs back inside. We all burst out laughing.

Soon after the Jim incident, Tim and Tina Wilson, come out to get in the hot tub. They have brought a bucket of ice, glasses, a bottle of rum and a two-liter cola. Tim sits on the edge of the hot tub, enjoying being the only man as he pours strong drinks.

"To our first fun filled night," Tim says, raising his glass in a toast. We all clink our glasses and sip at our drinks. Damn, he made these strong. I bet he is hoping if he gets us drunk, we will all jump on him. The thought of us all tearing into Tim makes me laugh.

"Did you see Jim when you were coming down here?" Sue asks, grinning from ear to ear.

"We saw him running up the stairs. Were you mean to him?" Tina accuses, getting a little of that school teacher tone to her voice.

24

"His body got a little out of control when he was watching us in the hot tub," Sue laughs.

Tina blushes, and we all laugh at Jim's expense.

"Have any of you ever ridden before?" Tim asks.

"I am an expert ride. At least that is what I have been told," Sue teases.

Rachel pushes Sue in the arm and laughs along with us. I see the look in Tim's eye and I think he is fantasizing about riding Sue. I figure I should switch the course of this conversation a little.

"I came here to learn how to ride a horse. I have only ridden one at a fair when I was little and that horse was being led. So this will be my first time truly riding horses," I interject.

"Tina and I have been riding many times. It is a good feeling to be in control of such a powerful beast," Tim says, looking a little too long at Sue.

"Oh, I love to ride. It is a wonderful way to see nature. I also love the horses, most are so gentle and smart. I like to brush them down after a good ride and feed them a treat like a molasses cake or an apple. I think it is funny how they can pick their treat out of your hand with their lips," Tina confesses obviously really in love with horses.

"Sue and I do not really know how to ride horses. I thought it would be fun and we could get a tan too," Rachel says rubbing Sue's back.

Tim fills up our glasses and we all sip and chat some more.

"What time was it when you came out?" I ask.

"It was just after midnight," Tina says.

"The night is young. Here, have another drink," Tim says, even though my drink is already almost full.

"Ahhh!" Tina screams and spills most of her drink as she jumps to her feet.

Most of us jump at Tina's scream, including me. She points and out in the darkness there is a figure walking this way. He soon enters the light. It is an old cowboy, maybe in his sixties. He is holding a tin can in one hand and an old fashion can opener in the other.

"Sorry to startle you, ma'am. My name is Corky. I work out yonder in the barn mostly. Mr. Toleson asked me to check on you before I hit the sack. Is there anything I can get fer y'all?" Corky says.

We all look at each other and everyone is trying not to laugh. Tina's cheeks are red from embarrassment and rum.

"No, I think we are good. Thanks for checking on us," I reply.

"Ok, well, I'll leave you young'uns to your frivolity. I'm a'goin down by the crick to eat me some peaches before hittin the hay. Hope y'all have a gay old time of it," Corky says, moseying off out into the night.

We all look at each other and burst out laughing. I know Corky must hear our laughter because we could not hold it until he had a chance to get out of earshot.

"Man, that guy was creepy. Did you see that can opener? You could kill someone with that thing," Tina says, giving a little shiver.

"He seemed like a real cowboy. Did you see his teeth? Most of them were missing," Rachel chuckles, making us all start laughing again.

I think we are feeling the rum and just letting go. When you are around strangers you will probably never see again after your vacation, you can relax and be freer to take chances. I am totally free but these two couples will have witnesses, namely their partners. Therefore, they can relax but not as much, or their partner will call them on it back in the real world or bring up an embarrassing story about them to their friends back home.

We continue to chat and drink, having a good time. We're all starting to feel the liquor. It must be about one o'clock and I am thinking of calling it a night. The girls are starting to get a little frisky with some serious lip lockage. Tina is ready to go to bed but Tim is groping on her and trying to take her bikini top off.

Tina finally has enough and gets out of the hot tub. "Come on, Tim. Let's go to bed. Goodnight, Sue. Goodnight, Rachel. Goodnight, Becket."

"Ok, coming, dear," Tim says, looking longingly at the scene in the hot tub. Tim gets out and follows Tina inside.

"I thought we were going to see Tina's cute little breasts," Sue whispers, as she starts to kiss Rachel's neck.

I feel this is my cue to leave. I get out of the hot tub. Sue stops and looks at me.

"Three is not really a crowd, you know. You could join us?" Sue winks.

As I am about to answer, we are interrupted by screams coming from inside the house.

"Ahhh! Ahhh! Ahhh!" A female voice shrieks over and over from inside the house.

I grab my towel and dash inside. I figure Sue and Rachel will follow when they can. I hear the screams coming from upstairs so I run up the stairs. On the second floor, I see Tim and Tina standing in the hall. Tina is screaming and pointing into one of the guest rooms. Jim retreats from the room they are looking into and backs into the wall. Jim is sobbing and slides down the wall to the floor. Jim has totally lost it. I make my way to the guest room and as I pass Jim, I notice he is covered in blood.

In the room, someone butchered John. There are blood splatters on most of the walls. John's eyes have been cut out and I do not see them in the room. His throat has been cut through his windpipe all the way

 28

to his spine. His stomach was sliced open and his intestines have fallen out. It is a true horror scene.

On the wall, written in blood, is the number 1 and a message. It looks like it might have been written using a finger dipped in John's blood.

"As the hours die, so shall you!" the message in blood reads.

Tina is now on the floor with Tim holding her. She has mostly stopped screaming. Jim is in the fetal position rocking back and forth on his side. I back out of the room and pull the door shut. I am not sure why I am so calm. I guess someone has to be. I also do not feel any danger. I would know if I was in immediate danger. The hair on the back of my neck always stands up when I feel threatened.

Sue and Rachel come into view from the stairs and walk over to us. Rachel sees the blood on Jim and turns on nurse mode. She approaches Jim and tries to calm him down while she looks to see if he is hurt. She soon looks up at the rest of us.

"This is not Jim's blood," Rachel says, looking at the closed door to John's room.

"It is John's blood. He is dead," I say. Sue looks more interested than scared. Both Tina and Jim renew their crying after hearing my words. Rachel gets up and reaches for John's door but I get in the way. "We need to call the police."

"Are you sure he is dead, Becket? I should check," Rachel insists, reaching for the door.

"Oh, I am sure. I would not recommend looking in there," I say as I move out of the way.

Sue moves over so she can see when Rachel opens the door. Rachel freaks at the sight of John's body. I push Rachel to the side so I can shut the door again.

"Who did it?" Sue says, looking at Jim.

"We are not sure. Let's go call the police," I say, heading downstairs.

The rooms do not have phones and my cell does not get a signal out here. I did see a phone in the living room downstairs, so I head for it. Sue follows me down the stairs. I can't believe we are still in our bathing suits. It would make me laugh a little, but then I think about John's butchered body upstairs and the smile leaves me.

We make it to the phone but there is no dial tone. I try the phone anyway but nothing happens.

"Let's look for another phone and wake the Tolesons. You would think they would have heard Tina's screams," I say.

We walk over to the Toleson's door and knock. Then Sue bangs on it. Sue tries the door after a minute of knocking but it is locked. We go over to the kitchen door and try that door. It is also locked. Sue gets pissed and picks up a log sitting next to the fireplace and starts hammering on the Toleson's door. It is damn loud and could wake the dead.

Tim and Tina come downstairs to see what all the noise is about. Sue decides enough is enough so she

 30

breaks off the door handle with the log and gets the door open. We all walk into a small living room. I see a phone but it does not work either. Tim sees a gun rack on the wall and goes over to get one. He takes down a deer rifle and checks it for ammunition. It has a couple shells in it. He looks around and finds a box of shells to load it. There are two other rifles in the gun rack.

There is another door opposite the one we just came in. Sue moves to that door and it is also locked. She smashes off the handle and gets the door open. We enter the Toleson's bedroom. It has a queen size bed that looks slept in.

"Where the hell are the Tolesons?" Rachel asks, from behind us making us jump.

"We don't know. Not here. The ranch hands sleep out in one of those outbuildings. Let's go find them," I say.

"Where is Jim?" Tina asks.

"I got him into his room and came to see what all the pounding was about," Rachel says.

"He might be the killer," Tim says, heading out to go find Jim with Tina in tow.

Sue goes over and takes down a gun. She rubs the barrel excitedly. I get a little freaked out by her actions so I take the other rifle. We both load them and head upstairs. Before we get to the stairs, we hear the familiar screeching of Tina.

Sue, Rachel and I tear up the stairs. Tina is screaming pointing into Jim's room this time as Tim desperately tries to calm her down. We rush over to them and look through the door. Jim has been decapitated. His body is lying on the bed, in the fetal position, with his back to the door. His head has been placed on the foot of the bed facing the door. His eyes are missing. They have been gouged out. Above the body on the wall is the number 2, again drawn in blood.

I am officially freaked out. I can feel the hair on the back of my neck stand up ever so slightly, meaning danger is near but not immediate. I have always been able to tell when I am in danger. We are being hunted.

"Maybe it is the Tolesons doing this. What the hell do we do?" Rachel asks, beginning to panic.

No one speaks up so I give my opinion. "First, we stay together. We have three rifles and strength in numbers. Second, let's find a working phone or try the bunk house to see if any of the ranch hands are around." I say, trying to convince myself as much as them.

I watch them nod their heads in agreement. We head back downstairs and go to the kitchen door. Sue, our expert burglar, smashes off the door handle with her log and gets us inside. The kitchen does have a phone but it also does not work. We look around, I see that there is a wooden knife block for large cutting knives. One of the larger knife slots is empty. I point this out to everyone.

"Oh my god, oh my god, we are all going to die," Tina shouts, falling to the floor crying.

"Let's try the bunk house. Tim, get your wife on her feet. We need to move," I say, heading out into the living room. Just then, the clock on the wall chimes the quarter hour and I look at it. It is 2:15 a.m. in the morning. The writing on the wall said, "As the hours die, so shall you". Jim died right about 1 a.m. John died right after 2 a.m. Maybe someone else will die right around 3 a.m.

"We need to hurry. Let's go," I say, heading to the front door.

I wait for Tim and Tina to catch up before opening the door. We all walk out on the front porch and look around. It looks quite enough out here. There is a light on the barn that gives us good vision. I lead the way with my rifle up. We head over to the bunkhouse and Sue knocks hard on the door with the butt of her rifle. When no answer comes, Sue tries the door and it opens. Inside are six bunks. Only two of them appear to have been slept in. We look around and find a phone but it does not work.

"Let's sit down and think. It looks like the Toleson's and their ranch hands may be involved. Even if they are not, they are not around to help. So we must assume we are on our own. What do we do?" I ask.

"We can steal a car and drive the hell out of this god forsaken place," Sue says.

"Ok, we need keys. Everyone search this room for keys." We look around but do not come up with any keys.

"Ah, damn it, let's hotwire one," Sue says, getting to her feet.

"Can you do that?" I ask.

"I have seen it done a couple times. It's worth a shot," Sue says.

"Well it's better than doing nothing. Lead the way," I say.

We all go back out into the night and head over to the carport. There is a truck and a four-door car. The truck is older and open so Sue tries that one. She gets under the steering column and has quite a hard time with getting to the wires she wants. All I can think is that it is getting closer to 3 a.m. all the time.

"I am really cold," Tina shivers.

We are all mostly naked out in the night with just our damp bathing suits on. We have been running on adrenalin but now that we have stopped to wait for Sue, it is wearing off. I am also cold. It has to be in the low sixties to maybe fifties and getting colder all the time. I know we are going to have to get inside soon.

"God damn, son of a bitch," Sue curses, coming out from under the steering column.

She pops the hood and looks at the engine.

 34

"I knew I was doing it right. The damn battery is gone," Sue says.

Sue walks over to the car and finds that its battery is also missing. She frantically goes over to the tractors, checking them one by one. All are missing batteries.

"All the batteries are gone. What now?" Sue asks.

"Let's go back inside and get some warmer clothes on. We are going to freeze out here. I would also really like to get some real shoes on. These flip flops are not made for walking around like this," I say heading into the ranch house.

We go inside, I notice it is ten till 3 a.m. We make our way up the stairs and to the third floor.

"Leave your doors open and get changed as quickly as you can," I say, going into my room.

I have my rifle ready and sweep the room before I go to my bag for clothes. I even look under the bed before changing. When I am dressed, I go across the hall, Sue is finishing up by putting on some nice black leather boots. I notice Rachel is not in the room.

"Where is Rachel?" I ask Sue.

"She had to go pee," Sue says, pulling on her other boot.

I walk down the hall and look into Tina and Tim's room. They are dressed but Tina is still brushing her hair. I guess brushing your hair is part of getting dressed and it is a normal thing to do. I figure it calms her to do the normal things especially when everything is anything but normal.

I knock on the bathroom door but there is no answer. Sue is walking down the hallway towards me. I try the door and it is locked. I pound on the door and Sue runs the rest of the way to join me. Sue shakes the door violently and I see blood pooling out under the door. I go into Tim and Tina's room and get a sturdy chair. I get Sue to move and smash the handle off the bathroom door. Sue opens the door and we see Rachel sitting on the toilet as if she is still peeing but missing her head. At first, I do not see the head at all but then I find it in the shower looking at me but without any eyes. Why do they take the eyes? On the shower curtain is the number 3 drawn in blood.

This time Tina does not scream. I think she is in shock. She goes where Tim guides her but does not move on her own, or speak at all.

I look around the bathroom and even check the window, which is locked. That means that whoever did this killed Rachel and walked out of the bathroom without Tim or Tina seeing or hearing anything. This is a quick, quiet killer.

"Let's go downstairs and hole up in the living room. There is a television and a fireplace we can light. We will just stay together and everything will be ok," I say, not really even believing myself.

We go downstairs. Tim puts Tina down on a couch and then works on getting a fire started. Sue flips on the TV but there is only static noise. There is a DVD player and some movies. She flips through the movies and picks out a comedy with that one fat guy, oh, I forget his name. Tim manages to get a fire going and we watch the movie. I know it is stupid to sit here but I don't know what else to do and it is calming to do something normal. Time passes. Every time the clock strikes on the quarter hour, I get a little bit more anxious. When the clock signals it is 3:45 a.m. I get up and go look at the stairs with the rife in my hand. I stay in sight of the others as I walk around looking out windows. I hear a door open and turn around to see Sue at the kitchen door.

"I'm hungry, anyone else want anything?" Sue asks, as she steps through the door.

"Wait!" I yell, as I run over to the kitchen door.

The door slams shut before I can get there and I hear a large thud as something big hits the door. I push upon the door but something is in the way.

"Tim, get over here and help me!" I yell as I shove on the kitchen door.

I get the door open just a little and can see there is movement in the kitchen. The hair on the back of my neck stands straight up and I know there is immediate danger to me. I stop pushing and wait for Tim to come over and help. I let Tim press and the tingling of danger goes away.

Tim finally gets the door pushed open and it is Sue's body in front of the door. She has been stabbed through the heart, her neck sliced and her eyes cut out. Written on the wall in blood is a message next to a larger number 4.

"Now fight without the light," the message in blood reads.

Just then, the power goes out. The only glow we have is coming from the fireplace. Tim and I go back to Tina who is still lying on the couch.

"Well what the hell do we do now?" Tim asks, looking at his near comatose wife.

"I don't know. Let's try to think of something," I say, racking my own brain for ideas.

"I can ride. How about I get a horse and ride for help?" Tim asks.

"That might work. I don't think you would get to help before Tina and I were past the point of needing it. Maybe we could all ride out of here. You could tie a horse to yours and Tina and I could ride it. If she does not snap out of this, I could just hold on to her. We might not be able to go as fast but we could get away from here," I say, looking at Tim.

"Hell it's worth a try. Anything is better than sitting here waiting to die," Tim says, as he starts to get Tina to her feet.

"Wait, we need some light. See if you can find a flashlight or something," I say.

Tim and I look all around the living room but only find two candles and a lighter. We get Tina up and search the Toleson's room using a candle for light. We find a lantern about half full of oil. The clock chimes 4:15 a.m. I know we need to hurry.

"This will have to do. Let's go."

I light the lantern and lead the way. We go outside and look into the darkness. There is no moon so we cannot see anything but what our lantern illuminates. I think this might be a bad idea but we have to get out of here. I hope I can stay on a horse with Tina.

We slowly walk out to the stables. When we get close, we can hear the horses getting jumpy. Tim sits Tina in a chair and starts saddling a horse. It is pretty involved and takes time we do not have. Then he saddles another horse and we are ready to give it a try. Tina is still in total shock. We get Tina on a horse then Tim helps me get on behind her. He ties a rope from our horse to his own. He has the lantern so he can somewhat see the road. We ride out of the stables. I just hold on to Tina and the horse for dear life. Tina is dead weight and not responsive at all. We ride for maybe five minutes and I think we are going to make it. God, I will be glad to get out of this place. I know I am never coming out to one of these ranches again. I still wonder who killed all those people.

"What the hell? Run it's a little...!" Is all Tim yells as the lantern falls to the ground and goes out.

Tim's horse makes a terrible sound and there is a sudden jerk on the rope tied to our horse. I cannot see a thing but I can smell blood. Tim and his horse must be dead. There is no sound coming from the darkness ahead. Tina is still in shock and we are sitting on a horse just down the road from the ranch house, I think. Hell, I do not really know where we are. It is so dark, I cannot see a thing. I put my fingers to work on the knot that ties our horse to Tim's horse. I get it undone and gently kick the horse. The horse starts walking but where it is going I have no idea. The horse walks for a few minutes until I can see light up ahead. The horse walks closer and I can see it is the light of the fireplace showing through the window of the ranch house. The horse just went the one place it knows best, home.

We sit on the horse and I try to think of what to do. Then I hear a noise coming from one of the out buildings. I look but cannot see anything. I sit very still and listen. Tina stiffens in front of me so I know she heard it too. It sounds like a small girl crying for her mother.

Tina gets off the horse and starts stumbling towards the child's cry in the dark. I get down and light one of the candles with the lighter we found. I follow along after Tina. The child's pleas take us to a small storage shed next to the ranch house. Tina opens the door and there is a young girl in a nightgown huddled in the corner calling for her mother. She is wrapped in a blanket and clutching a doll. The girl must be about six years old. She has shoulder length blond hair and a dirty face. Tina goes to her and hugs her. Tina and the child sit together in the corner as I try to figure out what to do.

"I'm Tina. What's your name?" Tina whispers.

"Lilly. Where's my mommy?" Lilly asks.

"Is Anny your mother?" Tina asks.

"Do you know my mommy?" Lilly asks.

"Yes, we know your mommy. How did you get out here?" Tina asks.

"I was asleep in bed and I heard screaming. My mommy wrapped me in a blanket and brought me here. She told me to never come out and be quiet. She would come and get me. She told me to go to sleep. So I went to sleep but woke up and want my mommy," Lilly explains.

"It's ok. We will stay with you until your mommy comes," Tina says.

I sit down and try to think about our situation. This building only has one door and no windows. Maybe we should just hold up in here until morning. I go and close the door. Then I push a chair up under the handle and go sit down. It is probably around 5:30 a.m. and the sun should come up just after 6 a.m. I do not think I will have ever been as happy to see a sunrise as I will today.

I have nothing to do but think. I look at Tina stroking Lilly's hair with her hand. Lilly's eyes are closed and she looks so peaceful. Lilly is stroking the hair of her doll just like Tina is stroking hers. Maybe we will get through this. I check my rifle and lay it across my lap.

Time passes and it has to be around 6 a.m. If the attack is coming, it should be soon. I watch the door for any kind of tampering. I look over at Lilly and Tina and I see Lilly is drawing in the dirt. It is hard to see in the candle light but it looks like she has drawn a circle in the dirt floor. Then she draws a loop off the circle making the number 6.

Oh my God, oh my God! I think about things I have seen and heard tonight. In the Toleson's bedroom, there was only the one bed. Where did Lilly sleep? Tim said "What the hell? Run, it's a little…!" What if he was saying, "Run, it's a little girl."

I slowly move the rifle so I can point it at Lilly. Before I get the barrel around Lilly breaks the silence.

"Will you be my mommy?" Lilly asks, looking at Tina.

"We will find your mommy, it will be ok," Tina says.

"I want a MOMMY!" Lilly screams, as she flips back the blanket and razes her arm with a large chopping knife in it.

Tina tries to throw Lilly off her. She is flailing and kicking at Lilly. Tina knocks Lilly's doll out of her hand and it lands in my lap. Lilly stabs the knife into Tina as I shoot Lilly with the rifle.

"BANG!"

Lilly keeps stabbing Tina even though I can see the bullet hole in her side. I shoot Lilly again.

"BANG!"

Tina is unmoving and I know she is dead. Lilly turns to me and bares her fangs. Her canines are very long and pointed. If I didn't know better, I would say she was a vampire. Lilly sinks her fangs into Tina and starts to drink her blood. I get the rifle ready to shoot again. I watch in horror as the bullet holes in Lilly ooze a little blood, expel the bullets and then heal over as if they were never there. The hair on the back of my neck stands straight up and I know I am going to die. I shoot Lilly again.

Lilly stops drinking and looks at me with blood-wet lips.

"Stop that, Mommy," Lilly hisses as she wipes her mouth off on Tina's shirt. "Can I have my dolly Mommy?" Lilly whispers, standing up and holding out her hand.

I look down at the doll in my lap and pick it up. When I touch it, I get a vision of the doll's past.

I see a beautiful woman with long blond hair holding the doll. She is clothed in a dress from maybe the turn of the century. She kneels down and hands the doll to Lilly. I can feel the love of the woman for Lilly and I know it is Lilly's real mom. Lilly is crying but takes the doll from her mother. I see a man grow fangs and feast on the mother's neck. I see the man rip

Lilly's moms head off. The man comes over to Lilly and bites her. The vision ends.

"Give me my DOLLY!" Lilly shouts.

I put the dolls head in front of the gun barrel and watch Lilly's reaction.

"NO! Don't hurt dolly. Please don't hurt dolly," Lilly begs.

I get up and move to the door still holding the doll's head in front of the gun. Lilly watches me and I can see she wants to hurt me. I kick at the chair under the door and almost fall. Lilly comes closer when I stumble but I point the gun with the doll head in front of it towards her and she stops. I manage to get the door open and I can see dawn is coming. I walk outside the shed backwards watching Lilly all the while. Lilly stands inside the shed watching me as the first rays of the sun wash over the valley. I feel the warmth of the sun and am so thankful for it. Lilly stands in the shadows of the shed glaring at me.

"I'm going to go to bed now. When I wake up, I am going to want my dolly. If I cannot find it, I will find you. Goodbye, Mommy," Lilly promises, and she shuts the door to the shed.

I throw the dolly over by the shed and head for the still saddled horse. I climb on and start it moving down the road. I am uncomfortable in the saddle but at least get the horse to walk the right way. I keep to the road and finally see a house late in the afternoon. I am sun burnt, smell of sweaty horse, sore all over, hungry and dead tired. I pull up outside the house and a farm hand comes out to help me. When I get down, I can barely walk. I hurt so badly from sitting on the horse too long.

"There have been some murders at the Goodrest Ranch. You need to call the police," I tell the hired man.

The farm hand helps me inside. He tells the women of the house what I said. She then calls the sheriff. After a minute, she hands me the phone.

"You say there have been murders at the Goodrest Ranch? How many?" The sheriff asks.

"At least six that I know of. You need to get out there before dark," I say.

"I am sending the closest deputies and ambulance now. Why before dark?" The sheriff asks.

I wonder how to answer that question. Should I tell them about the six-year-old vampire? That is probably not a good idea.

"All the power and phones are out. It will be easier to see in the daytime," I lie, telling only part of the reason.

"What is your name, miss?" the sheriff asks.

"Rebecca Shaw," I say.

"You stay there with the Matson's. Let me speak to Mrs. Matson again," the sheriff says.

I hand the phone to Mrs. Matson. She walks away talking on it. I spend the rest of the afternoon and much of the night with the Matsons. They feed me and let me rest. About midnight the sheriff comes by and takes me to his office. I sleep a little in the car and at his office.

The next morning the questioning starts. I get the idea that I am a suspect. They only find five bodies of the guests, Tina's body is never found. There is also no mention of a little girl by the sheriff, so I decide not to bring it up. The Toleson's and their ranch hands are found a couple days later, all dead in a gully. The only reason they were found at all is the buzzards led the searchers to them. All this time I have to stay in town at a shabby hotel and be available to answer questions. My things are brought to me from the ranch.

Two agents from the FBI even come in to interrogate me. They question me privately in my hotel room and ask some interesting questions.

"You mentioned seeing a ranch hand named Corky. Is that correct?" Agent Smith asks.

"Yes, he asked us if we needed anything when we were in the hot tub."

"You stated that he was holding a can of peaches and an old-fashioned can opener. Is that correct?" Agent Smith questions.

"Yes," I say, wondering what this has to do with anything.

"How was he dressed?" Agent Smith asks.

"In work clothes. I guess they were of a pretty old style. He looked to be pretty dirty," I say, thinking this is a strange query.

Agent Smith shows me a black and white photo of a man that looks to be Corky. The photo is very old and faded.

"Is this the man you saw?" Agent Smith asks.

"Yes, that's him. Why do you ask?"

"No one else around here has ever heard of a Mr. Corky at the Toleson's or anywhere else."

"Then how do you have a picture of him?" I ask, perplexed.

"This picture is from an old case. Your case has some similarities so we brought the picture to show you," Agent Smith replies.

"What old case?"

"Sorry but we need to move ahead with the questions. Did you see a little girl at the ranch?"

"Did the Toleson's have a daughter?" I ask, thinking maybe I was wrong and Lilly was the Toleson's vampire daughter.

"The Toleson's did not have any children. Did you see a little girl at the ranch?"

"Yes," I say.

"What did she look like?" Agent Smith asks.

"She was 5 or 6 years old with shoulder length blond hair. She always carried a doll with her."

"What was her name?"

"Lilly," I say.

"Did she hurt anyone?" Agent Smith asks.

"I'm pretty sure she killed them all," I confess.

"Why did you not tell this to the sheriff?"

"Because I did not think anyone would believe me. Hell, do you believe, me Agent Smith?"

"Yes, I believe you, Ms. Shaw."

"What? You believe me. Why?" I ask, wondering what the hell is going on.

"Because there are records of this sort of thing happening before in the area."

"Really, when?" I ask, wanting to know more about what happened.

"1898, 1914, 1936, 1963, 1981."

I don't know what to say.

"Did Lilly display any unusual abilities?" Agent Smith inquires.

"Well, she murdered six people when it was almost impossible to get to them. She must have been very quiet and fast. She had fangs like a vampire. She healed three bullet wounds right in front of my eyes. She drank Tina's blood," I say.

I watch as the two Agents look at each other and nod.

"The official story is Tina Wilson killed the Tolesons, their ranch hands and all their guests but one Rebecca Shaw. Here is your statement, already filled out to confirm that story. Please sign down here by the X," Agent Smith says.

"But you know that is not what really happened."

"What really happened is what the report says. What do you think people would say about you or us if we filed your version of the truth? This way people can go on living their normal lives. You can go back to your life and we can go on doing our job," Agent Smith says.

"What exactly is your job?" I ask, thinking this is way beyond what I thought the FBI did.

"That is a need to know issue, and frankly, it is better if you do not know. Now, sign the paper and you can be on your way," Agent Smith says.

I take the statement and sign it. The agents get up to leave with my statement.

"You are free to go. We will be in touch. Oh, and if you see Tina Wilson or Lilly again, especially at night, you might want to run," Agent Smith warns as he shuts the door to my hotel room.

Chapter Three: Choices

It has been a month since the worst vacation ever to the Goodrest Ranch. I have settled into my marketing job and it is going well. I think I like the music industry people more than the job. My work and life seem so normal compared to what I know exists out there in the dark.

The nightmares of drowning in blood have been much more frequent in the last month. They never truly went away since I touched Antal's cane but I was down to only having a nightmare every few months or so. This last month, I have had a nightmare about every other night. One of the most constant scenes in my nightmare is Lilly holding Tina's hand. They both have vampire fangs. I often see other images and events that happened at the Goodrest Ranch in my nightmares, but they always end with me drowning in blood. I know this is all related to touching Antal Degano's cane and the vision of blood.

One night after work, I go to dinner with some friends. I am always careful to be around a lot of people at night since my "vacation". I even have a top-of-the line security system for my apartment. I walk to my car with some friends and see a man watching me. At first, I am not sure who it is but he steps into the light and I can see it is Agent Smith. I get in my car and my friends go their own way. I start my car but sit and watch Agent Smith in my mirror. He walks up to my car and gets in the passenger side.

"Good evening, Ms. Shaw," Agent Smith says.

"Good evening, Agent Smith," I reply, thinking this can't be good.

"How have you been Ms. Shaw? Are you still having nightmares?" Agent Smith probes, looking at me like I am an interesting specimen not a person.

"Yes," I say cautiously, wondering how he knows about my nightmares.

"Maybe we could help make your nightmares go away. Would you like that Ms. Shaw?" Agent Smith asks, still studying my face.

"Of course I would like that, but I'm not too sure I would like the cure. What do you have in mind?" I frown. This guy is making me really nervous but I don't feel any danger sense.

"I am offering you a job Ms. Shaw," Agent Smith says.

"A job with whom? The FBI?" I hesitate.

"The FBI is part of it but we are a special branch. To everyone outside our group, you would appear to work for the FBI. Our branch deals in special cases like the one you were involved in," Agent Smith clarifies.

"So you want me to come to work for you and hunt down vampires and other supernatural creatures?" I chuckle, thinking this is crazy.

"Yes," Agent Smith replies matter-of-factly.

I can't believe this. I do not know what to say. He wants me to join his organization and hunt vampires. That is some crazy shit.

Agent Smith watches me as I think about his proposal. He hands me a cell phone.

"Keep this with you. It has my number in it. Give me a call if you decide to take my offer or you see any old friends," Agent Smith warns as he gets out of the car and walks into the shadows.

I feel my heart racing and notice my breathing quicken. I am really scared. I am scared of what might be out there in the dark. I am almost never scared. My ability to sense danger has made it so I have little fear of death. Nevertheless, I fear the unknown creatures of the night now. What the hell do I do? I can't live like this.

I drive home, constantly looking over my shoulder. I check every hiding place in my apartment before I start to settle down. I was already a little scared at night but after meeting with Agent Smith, I'm very scared. He seems to think I will be visited by Lilly and Tina. Maybe that is why I keep seeing them in my nightmares. I could be seeing them searching for me.

Just calm down, I tell myself. I am safe in my apartment. It will be ok. I really try to convince myself everything will be all right but it doesn't really work. I have gone through a life-changing event. I know for a fact that vampires exist. I have experienced an encounter with them first hand. Now that I think about it, I believe my vacation was not my first meeting with a vampire. I think that is why my nightmares about Lilly and Tina are linked to my vision from Antal Degano's cane and the vision of blood. I think Antal Degano was a vampire.

But, that would mean that Gran knew Antal Degano was a vampire. She said Antal was an honored guest and she respected him. It all fits together. Antal could not enter our house until he was invited. He was very young but held great power and respect. He was pale and dressed in an old fashioned style. Then there is his cane and the vision of blood.

I lie awake for much of the night, thinking about the old country and my horror-filled vacation. I think I am right about the vampire connection. It does mean that maybe not all vampires are bad or monsters. On the other hand, maybe Antal was bad and my Gran just did not know. His cane had certainly seen some serious violence to cause my blood-filled vision. I wish I remembered more of the visions from the cane besides being drowned in blood. I'm sure I must have seen something that would give me insight into Antal Degano.

The next day I go to work and talk to my friends but it is no good. All I can think about is vampires and Agent Smith. I bet he knew it would just take me some time to get used to the idea. Damn, what the hell am I going to do now? I could go back to Gran's house and talk to her about Antal and my vacation. I'm not sure that is the best course of action. Antal might have a special mission for me and I might never leave the valley again. I think I will see what Agent Smith has to offer. The information and training I can get from Agent Smith will serve me well when I finally do decide to go back to visit Gran and Antal Degano.

I call Agent Smith and tell him I would like to discuss his job offer. He gives me an address in Seattle to meet him. The address leads me down to the shipping docks and a large warehouse. I walk into warehouse number twelve and find an empty building. When Agent Smith walks in, I do not feel in danger, so I try to remain calm.

"What do you want to know?" Agent Smith asks.

"Do we hunt supernatural things or just observe them? Is this about information gathering or destruction?" I ask, concerned about my safety.

"We do both. In the end, it is mostly investigating after the fact. However, sometimes there is a true threat to the population and we get involved early enough to neutralize the threat. We do not kill supernaturals on sight, not that it is that easy to kill most of them." Agent Smith explains.

"How long have you been with this organization?" I ask, deciding that Agent Smith is probably in his mid-thirties.

"Seven years. I was an Army Ranger before that for six years," Agent Smith reveals, which tells me a lot about his demeanor.

"Why are you offering me this job?" I can't help but wonder why they want me.

"Our controller believes in recruiting people who have already encountered the supernatural. We have found that it is hard to train for this kind of work. You can give someone the best training available but if they cannot handle the fact that vampires are real, they are worthless to us and can even become a liability in extreme cases. You have proven yourself fairly calm in an unbelievable situation, thus making you a prime candidate for our organization. We have also taken the last month to do an extensive background check on you. You speak multiple languages, have a degree in marketing, are very physically fit, you are young and you have a politically powerful family on your father's side and a very interesting old world family on your mother's side," Agent Smith explains.

"So what is the catch?" I ask skeptically.

"You will have to lie to everyone about what you really do and often even what your name is. You will sever ties with pretty much every friend you have ever made and will have limited contact with your family. Your true identity will become a secret and hidden away so well that even you would have trouble convincing people you ever existed. You will live under a variety of false identities. It will be hard for you to maintain good friends or relationships. We travel a lot and at a moment's notice. You could be gone for days or even weeks. Sometimes the assignments can be deadly, but that is not the norm. You will have to fill out reports and be held accountable for your actions. It is definitely a life changing decision and not a decision you can easily walk away from once you have joined. But you will be trained and educated in what little we know about the supernatural. I think our organization exists because we stay in the shadows and do not bite off more than we can chew. It will be interesting and exciting work but also can be dangerous and scary," Agent Smith says.

"So right now I could walk away and that would be the end of it?" I say, thinking for a brief moment that it might be the best thing to do.

"Yes. I do not think you are stupid enough to go talking about us or what happened at the Goodrest Ranch. Even if you did talk, who would believe you? You have no evidence, a crazy story and you even signed a sworn statement to the official story for the authorities. We would also discredit you and you would lose your credibility, your job and your friends. I have seen it happen to others, so don't be stupid," Agent Smith warns.

"If I say yes, what happens?" I ask.

"You will go through training under your real name. You will be sent to the FBI New Agent training facility in Quantico and go through the regular twenty-one week program. Then you will attend some advanced courses set aside for CIA and NSA agents for another sixteen weeks, probably under a false name. After that, you will be assigned to a government post, most likely in the FBI to start. The post will be in something like public relations working on the image of the FBI in a small, out of the way office. The PR job will be a cover for those family and friends you continue to keep in contact with. You will actually work out of one of our organization's field offices. From there, you will undergo even more training and learn a lot about the supernatural. After that, you will be assigned cases to work and truly start your career as an agent investigating the supernatural," Agent Smith explains.

"I feel that I am backed into a corner. I look around corners and wonder what lurks in the darkness. I have nightmares of Lilly and Tina coming for me. I do not think I can live a normal life being scared all the time but what you are offering is not normal either. I think if I learned more about the supernatural and knew how to combat it, then the fear would go away or at least be controllable," I confide.

"I cannot tell you what to do. I can tell you I understand your situation a little. Most of the Agents in our organization have had similar feelings at one time or another. Nevertheless, don't be fooled into thinking the other agents will be your best friends and always help you through things. Our experiences with the supernatural often have a negative effect on us. Some of us deal with the experiences badly and become withdrawn or even antisocial. Do not get me wrong, some of the agents will be great but many will not be your friends. Agents also move around a lot. You may even be forced to move to a new field office. Sometimes this is done because you need new identities, sometimes because your expertise might be needed elsewhere. However, what it all boils down to is that you will not even know if you can trust a fellow agent. Sure, they will back you up in the field but I would not share my personal lives with very many of them. Moreover, don't go thinking I am some great guy for telling you the truth and I will be your friend. I've been told I can be a real ass"

"You're not a very good salesman, Agent Smith. You paint a pretty bleak picture," I admit, looking at him and trying to figure out if I can even trust him.

"I don't like this part of the job. I wish that when I was recruited, someone had told me the things I am telling you. I try to fool myself into believing I would have turned down the job, but I was all 'yes, sir, for my country, sir' back then. They could have told me I would die in a year and I still would have joined," Agent Smith says, pausing for a moment remembering the past. "Someday you may be in my shoes recruiting a Norm. A Norm is what we call normal people who live in happy ignorance about the existence of the supernatural. What would you tell that recruit? That it is all glamour and fast cars? That you will be serving mankind? Or that you could be gutted and left for dead? I try and tell recruits the answers to their questions and what I would have liked to have known," Agent Smith continues, looking grim but determined.

"If you take this job, make sure it is for the right reasons because there is no going back. You will learn things that few in the world do. Those things can weigh on your soul if you are not careful. You can also never forget what you already learned and witnessed. You came out of a horrifying experience involving a vampire. Therefore, you have a strong will, but to face experiences like that every day, you need to be very strong. We have techniques and counselors to help you, but in the end, a lot of it comes down to what you are made of," Agent Smith admits.

"I told you I was an Army Ranger for six years. During that time, I killed thirty-two people. Six were up close and personal with a knife or my bare hands. Two were kids and three were women, all from the same grenade I threw into a house. I saw eight of my buddies die. Those experiences weigh on my soul and I carry them with me every day and night. Nevertheless, they were nothing compared to my encounters with the supernatural. I deal with it by being cold and removed emotionally. I am not saying that is the best way, just the defense mechanism I use to keep sane enough to keep doing my job. Other people handle the stress differently. If you join us, you will have to find what works for you," Agent Smith concludes.

If I do this, I will end up killing people and supernaturals. I will hunt people and supernaturals. I will lock them away, maybe for life. I bet this organization also experiments on supernaturals. I would be assigned to cases and have to work them if I like the situation or not. Am I willing to do all that? What am I trying to get out of this?

Sure, it would be cool to have a badge and some government authority, but I bet the supernaturals are not going to give a rat's ass about my stupid badge. Hell, the little vampire hellion Lilly could have gutted me where I stood and there was nothing I could do about it. My gifts of danger sense will probably be working overtime on this job. My ability to see visions from objects would be very useful but what if I fall into another vision and go into a coma again or die. I do not know what to do.

"I'd like more time to make sure I am making the right choice but I don't want to live my normal life either. I don't feel safe anymore," I admit.

"The FBI would be glad to have you, Ms. Shaw, if you worked for our organization or not. How about I

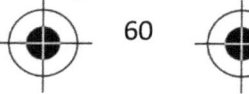

push the paperwork through and get you a job with the FBI in the PR department. You will still have to go through the same New Agent Training. That will give you twenty-one weeks of training to make up your mind. You should feel safer living on campus in Quantico. What do you think about that idea?" Agent Smith asks.

"That sounds like a good idea. I think I might like working for the FBI even if I decide not to join your organization. By the way, what organization do you work for?" I ask.

"I cannot tell you that. I figure you understand. It would not be secret if we talked about it. The name is only used internally anyway. We always work under the guise of some other organization like the FBI, CIA, NSA/CSS, SIS, and Interpol. You get the idea."

"You will be contacted by a recruiter in a day or two. They will get with you to finish filling out your application and get you set up to start on your training. Remember, you must assume that everyone you meet from now on is who they say they are and have no idea about the supernatural. You will officially be hired by the FBI to work in PR. If you want to switch to join our organization call me on the phone I gave you. Otherwise, this will be goodbye for us, Ms. Shaw. I wish you peace of mind in whatever path you choose," Agent Smith vows and he offers me his hand.

"It sure was interesting meeting you. I wish you luck out there doing whatever you do," I say honestly, as I shake his hand.

With our goodbyes said, Agent Smith turns and leaves. I watch him go and wonder where he is going. What supernatural thing he is going to investigate next. I like marketing and public relations but I don't think I will be satisfied with just that after all I have been through. I think I have caught the bug to be out in the field. Well, time will tell, for now I am going to be a "Secret Agent Man," I think as I start to sing that song to myself.

Chapter Four:
Hunted

Agent Smith is true to his word. The next day, I get a call from the local FBI office they have scheduled an appointment for me this afternoon. I spend the whole afternoon filling out paperwork and signing forms. I am finger printed and my photo taken. Hell, they even do a complete physical with blood and urine analysis. At the end of the day, I am told my plane will leave for Quantico on Saturday, which is just two days away.

"I have not even given notice to my job," I kind of say to myself as much as to Agent Bean who is helping me fill out paperwork.

"It says in your file that your former employer has been officially notified of your departure. That's funny, it says that was done today. Your whole file is such a mess. The memo said your first application that we received six months ago was misplaced and that is why there has been the last minute rush," Agent Bean complains.

"You sound like you just found out you were going into training and got the job. The government is slow and takes months to do all the appropriate things to hire a new person," Agent Bean reveals.

I just kind of laugh to myself, because I did just decide to join the FBI yesterday. Agent Smith must have really pulled some strings to make this happen so fast. I had better be careful what I say. I guess I applied six months ago and got the acceptance letter a couple months ago. Well that will not matter much, in a few days I will be out of here and in training.

"Thank you for taking all this time to straighten out my records, Agent Bean," I say.

"Normally, you would have just been bumped to the next training class, but a request came from up high to have your file pushed through. You must have some friends in high places," Agent Bean sighs.

We finish up and I go home to pack. I have tons of paperwork to read through before I leave. I have a couple messages on my phone from work friends all wondering what is going on. They say the boss told them I got a government job and was leaving immediately. My cubicle was all packed up and taken away. About the time I finish listening to my messages, I hear a knock on the door. I look through the peephole and see it is what looks to be a couple of delivery guys with boxes. I open the door and they show me FBI badges. They are Agent Weis and Agent Price.

"Ms. Shaw?" Agent Weis asks.

"Yes," I say.

"These are the contents of your cubicle from your former place of work. May we put them inside for you?" Agent Weis inquires.

"Yes please, over there," I suggest, pointing to a spot.

The agents come in and put the boxes in neat stacks.

"We have been assigned to you until you enter the training facility in Quantico. One of us will stay with you in your apartment and the other will roam nearby. Do you understand?" Agent Weis explains.

"Yes, but I have errands and things I must do before I leave," I admit.

"We understand ma'am. We will try to stay in the background as much as possible but where you go, we go. Those are our orders. We are not leaving your side until you are through the gates of Quantico and settled in your room. We understand that you have had threats against your life and we take such things very seriously," Agent Weis insists.

"Are you out of the Seattle office?" I wonder.

"No, we do special missions that take us all over the country. You must rate to get us pulled from our last assignment in the middle of the night so we could get here ASAP. We are professionals in the field who specialize in security and wet work, not desk jocks, ma'am," Agent Weis says proudly.

Wet work, hum…I have heard of that before. It is another way of saying assassinations. These guys must kill people for the government. Guess I better be nice to them. "Make yourselves at home," I say, shutting the door with both of them inside my apartment.

Agent Smith must be protecting me. Maybe he feels there is a real threat or more likely, he just wants me to feel safe. Either way it will be an interesting couple of days.

They walk through the apartment looking it over. I guess they are trying to figure out lines of fire and possible exits. Agent Price does make himself at home. He flops on the couch and turns on the TV. A news report is on.

"The fire started early this morning and has been difficult to contain. The private club Eros has been a staple in the alternative community for years. The firefighters on site tell me Eros is beyond saving and they are concentrating on making sure the fire does not spread. The bar was closed at the time the fire started. It is now believed that the club's owner, Sapphire Stone, and local band legend, Jay Zeal, were trapped inside by the fire and are presumed dead," the reporter says.

****

Agent Weis and Agent Price go with me everywhere over the next couple of days. They are heavily armed and have their own car, even though one of them rides with me all the time. They do not ask questions. I guess they just do not care or they have been told not to ask. They mostly just want to know where we are going and whom we are meeting so they can plan the best way to cover me at all times. They are professionals and I do feel safer having them around.

I have to go to dinner with my parents before I leave town. I call my dad and tell him my plan to join the FBI. He has a small fit on the phone but gets over it quickly. I make sure dad will tell my mother so she knows before I come over for dinner. Another problem besides my sudden plan to leave for FBI training is Agent Weis and Agent Price refuse to let me go to dinner alone. I convince Agent Weis to play my FBI boyfriend who got me into the idea of joining. From the look on Agent Weis's face, I think he would rather be facing down armed gunmen than come to my family dinner.

"Oh, Rebecca, you look nice tonight. Who is your friend?" My mom interrogates as she greets us at the door.

My dad comes up in time to hear my mom's question. Neither of them are pleased I brought a date. I am sure they wanted some alone time with me to try to talk me out of joining the FBI.

"This is Agent Weis with the FBI. He's my date," I announce.

"Good evening, ma'am. Good evening sir," Agent Weis says to my mom and dad as he shakes their hands.

"Well, come in and sit down, dinner is almost ready. Rebecca, you can help me in the kitchen," my mom says dragging me off by the arm to the kitchen.

Agent Weis is not too excited about leaving my side or going into the den with my father.

"Why did you bring that agent with you, Rebecca? You know your father and I wanted to talk to you about your sudden decision. Sue Hatton called me and said she heard government men came to your office and took all your stuff. What is this all about?" my Mom asks.

"Agent Weis is cool and we can talk in front of him. He will not butt into our conversation. So let's just talk in front of him and Dad so I do not have to go off privately and have all these conversations twice," I protest heading back out to the den.

"Well, maybe we will feel uncomfortable around your agent friend. Did you ever think of that, Rebecca?" My mom accuses, following me into the den.

"I know this is awkward but Weis is here and he is going to stay. Let's just talk in front of him. He knows what is going on anyway," I admit.

In the end, I start to explain. "Mom asked why all my personal possessions were packed up at my office by government men. It was done to help me. I got a spot in the training session that starts on Monday. I was not supposed to go for a month. So the FBI stepped in to help me get my affairs in order early.

I'm sorry if it causes anyone a problem. The stuff from my office has already been delivered to my apartment. Ok, next question," I say, just wanting to get this over with so we can try to enjoy the rest of the night.

"Why are you joining the FBI?" My dad asks.

"I feel vulnerable after what happened at the Goodrest Ranch. Maybe if I'd had some proper training not all those people would have died. Anyway, I have only signed up to work in the Public Relations department, so I'm not going into fieldwork. It will be an office job with a lot of travel. I am twenty-one years old it will be good for me," I admit.

I can see noticeable relief on my parents face when I tell them I'm not doing fieldwork.

"Do you blame yourself for the deaths of those people at that ranch?" my mom asks.

"No, not at all. That was a very bad situation. I'm lucky to be alive. I just want to feel safer. I think getting FBI training will provide that," I deflect

"This all seems so sudden," my mom says.

"I know I should have talked to you about it but I didn't know if I would even be accepted. I have been having nightmares about the events on the ranch since it happened. I just need to do something and this seems like the best option. If this spot had not opened up at the last minute, we would have had more time, but in the end, I still would have joined. I need this opportunity to give me some firm ground I can stand on again. Everything has been too shaky for me since the ranch," I admit.

"How long is your training?" my dad asks.

"Twenty one weeks, but I may sign up for some extra instruction which will add another sixteen weeks or so onto that," I inform.

"Will you learn how to use a gun?" my mom whispers.

"Yes, but you know Uncle Degano taught me how to shoot a rife when I was ten. My cousins and I used to hunt on Gran's and Uncle Degano's land every summer after that. So I already know how to shoot a rifle, just not a handgun. All FBI agents have to go through firearms training. If my PR campaigns are not working, I need to be able to make people feel good about the FBI at gunpoint. So having all this training should come in handy," I say in a flippant tone.

"Really, Rebecca! This is not a joke, it is life changing. You are going to be an Agent with the FBI even if it is in Public Relations. Are you sure this is the right thing to do?" my mom asks.

"No, I'm not absolutely sure. But I feel in my gut that it's what I need to do right now. You didn't really like that music magazine I was working at anyway. This job with the FBI will pay double my last job. I need to do this for me. Please just be happy for me," I plead looking at my parents.

"We are happy with you, baby girl. This is just real sudden and we want to make sure you are not

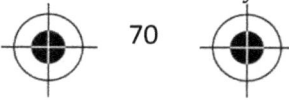

making a mistake. I know it has been hard for you since that horrible vacation at the ranch. If this is what you want, we will support you. You know I have connections in the government so if you ever need anything you let me know," my dad comforts, coming over and giving me a hug.

I glance at Agent Weis as he squirms uncomfortably. I smile at him as I hug my dad. He looks at me as if he is in pain. My mom comes over and hugs me, and I know it will be OK. They have accepted my decision and will support me now.

"Well I'm sure my meatloaf is well done by now. Everyone wash up and come into the dining room," my mother says walking off to the kitchen.

As we are on the way to the dinner table, I get close to Agent Weis and ask him a question.

"So how many guns did you bring into my father's house?" I wonder.

"Three guns, two knives and a garrote, but I'm not sure it is enough. Agent Price is outside just in case we need backup to cut up your mom's meatloaf," Agent Weis teases giving me a slight smile.

After having an eventful evening at my parent's house, Agent Weis and I drive home. He walks with me to my apartment. When we get to the door, I go to unlock it but it is ajar. I push on the door and it swings open. On the floor is a man in a security uniform from my security company decapitated. His head is sitting right inside the door facing me with missing eyes. There on the wall across from the open door is a giant number 7 drawn in blood. Agent Weis sees this and has a gun out instantly.

"We have to run now," I insist moving away from the open door as the hair on the back of my neck stands straight up warning me of danger from within my apartment.

"Code 99, I repeat code 99. We are coming down," Agent Weis calls to the air but I am sure Agent Price can hear him through a com system.

Agent Weis pushes me down the corridor towards the stairs, as he watches behind us. I know we are being chased as my danger sense is going crazy. I could die here and now.

"There is a little girl, a woman and an old man. They will take many bullets to stop. We have to run, not stand and fight," I explain as we start heading down the stairs.

We burst out the stairs door into the parking garage and Agent Price is standing next to his car with his gun drawn. He points his gun at something behind us over the roof of the car and starts firing over and over. Agent Weis pushes me towards the car, turns around, and unloads his clip into whatever is following us. The hair on the back of my neck is going crazy. I know Agent Weis is in the most danger. I want to turn and look but Agent Price yells at me.

"Get in the damn car, woman!" Agent Price screams as he continues to shoot.

I manage to enter the car. Agent Price gets in and squeals the tires out of there. I look back and see Agent Weis on the ground being literally ripped apart by Lilly and Tina. Lilly looks up at me still holding her dolly and yells, "MOMMY, come back Mommy!"

Agent Price keeps us moving and heads for the freeway. My danger sense has waned and I know we are ok for now. My phone rings and it is Agent Smith.

"Becket? Are you all right? The Agents I sent to cover you called in that you were compromised," Agent Smith asks.

"It was Lilly and Tina. They killed a security guard in my apartment and got Agent Weis. I am with Agent Price now in his car heading south. I am ok but shaken up. Agent Price is also unhurt," I relate, breathing hard as I'm still freaked out.

"I understand. I will send a cleanup crew to your apartment. You cannot go back there ever again. Stay with Agent Price, Becket, he will protect you. Let me speak to him please," Agent Smith asks.

I hand the phone to Agent Price and he says, "Yes, sir" a lot and then hands the phone back to me.

"You will fly out of Portland instead of Seattle. Agent Price will drive all night to get you to your flight. I do not think your old friends will be able to follow you that fast. You will also be flying under false names. Just go with it. I am sorry this happened to you. I felt the threat from your old friends was minimal or I would have protected you better," Agent Smith apologizes.

"I understand. I was just starting to like Agent Weis. He died right in front of me. As we were getting away in the car Lilly called me Mommy," I grimace.

There is a pause and I feel Agent Smith is thinking. "They may come after you again. It will be very difficult for them to get to you at Quantico. I will arrange to have your parents guarded for the next couple of weeks just in case. I do not think there will be any issue but I am sure it will make you feel better," Agent Smith reassures me.

"Thanks. I will feel better knowing my parents are being protected."

"Get some rest in the car if you can. You should be in Quantico by the end of the day tomorrow. Stay safe," Agent Smith says, then he disconnects the call.

"I don't want to know any more than I do. I am under strict orders to just do what I am told and ask no questions, but this just ain't right. Agent Weis was the best partner I ever had. That crazy little girl and woman took him down like he was a ragdoll. We must have shot them at least ten times each," Agent Price sighs and glances at me calming down a bit. "I'll do my best, don't worry about that. Try to get some sleep. I will get you to Quantico."

Agent Price is true to his word. We fly from Portland and make it to Quantico around dinnertime.

Agent Price walks me through security and to my room.

"I know you will do well here and I will expect it of you since Agent Weis gave his life to give you this chance. Make his memory proud by being as great as he was one day. I'll be watching you," Agent Price says, offering me his hand.

"Thank you. I will try and to live up to Agent Weis's example," I pledge as I push Agent Price's hand aside and give him a hug instead.

Agent Price returns the hug but I can tell he is uncomfortable about it. He waves goodbye and walks down the hallway and out of sight.

Chapter Five:
Training

By the end of my twenty-one weeks of training, I feel good about what I have learned. I never stepped off campus the whole time I was at Quantico. I used the extra time to study and practice for my courses. I did not make it to top of my class, but I did score third. I feel I am qualified for the PR job I was hired for and then some. I do not think I am as capable as Agent Weis but that will come in time. Sure, I can use my handgun proficiently and am excellent at hand to hand, but Agent Weis was much better and he did not stand a chance against a vampire. I know vampires are real and will probably be in my life no matter what I do. To feel safe, I need to join Agent Smith's organization. I will be put in dangerous situations in the field but my danger sense will warn me and I can prepare for them. This constant looking over my shoulder stuff is unnerving, and getting old. I'm going to call Agent Smith and confirm my extra training.

"Agent Smith?" I ask.

"Becket. So I hear you graduate from your training tomorrow. You were third in your class, not bad."

"Yep, right on all accounts. I guess you have been keeping tabs on me?"

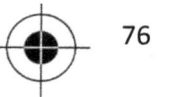

"I like to know about the lives of our potential recruits. So have you made a decision about joining us?"

"Yes. I want to go forward. I don't feel I have enough specialized knowledge to deal with old friends that may pop up eventually."

"Ok, I will make it happen. You will receive designated assignment papers before you leave Quantico. Still assume everyone you meet is who they say they are and nothing more. At the end of your training go to your assigned post and do your duties. I will contact you when it is time," Agent Smith says.

"I understand. Will it be long before you contact me?" I wonder.

"The timing will depend on a lot of things. It will not be more than six months and most likely much sooner. Up until the point I contact you and you agree to move forward, you can still pull the plug and just continue at your assigned job. So continue to think about what course is best for you. Enjoy the training. I might throw in a couple extra weeks of specialized training I think you could use. Talk to you when it is necessary," Agent Smith concludes as he ends the call.

When I joined the FBI, I thought it was all about handling kidnapping, counterfeiting, organized crime and crimes across state lines. The FBI does all those things but it is not their primary focus. Their primary focus is to stop terrorists and foreign spies. I never knew that before I joined the FBI. The mission of the

FBI reads: "To protect and defend the United States against terrorist and foreign intelligence threats, to uphold and enforce the criminal laws of the United States, and to provide leadership and criminal justice services to federal, state, municipal, and international agencies and partners."

Even though I have chosen to move into Agent Smith's organization, I am proud to have been given the opportunity to go through the FBI training. It really opened my eyes to what they do for the average citizen every day. I know there is corruption and bureaucracy but I still feel better knowing the FBI is out there watching out for the United States.

My parents come to graduation and I have dinner with them on the grounds afterwards.

"Do you know where you will be posted?" my dad asks.

"No, not yet. I am going to be doing some traveling and taking more instruction before I get a posting," I answer.

"I have heard several graduates telling their families and friend their posting. Is more training unusual?" my dad probes.

"Maybe a little, however, it's the government. They have their own way of doing things. I will know in a couple months," I clarify.

"Well, I have half a mind to call in some favors and get you posted close to home in Seattle," my dad threatens.

"No, please don't. I want to do this on my own. Maybe after my first rotation in a few years I will let you help, but right now let me handle things," I beg.

"Ok, I will stay out of it, but if you need anything you give me a call," my dad orders.

"I will, Dad. Thanks for the offer," I say.

"I am so proud of you making third in your class. You must have studied a lot more than in college. You never got all A's before," my mom teases.

"Ah, Mom, come on. I didn't do that bad in school. Beside, here, I lived in a dorm on a secure facility. I didn't have a lot else to do but study, but more than that, I really wanted to do well. It is important to me to succeed in the FBI," I confess.

"Well, I'm very proud of my little girl. You looked younger than most of the graduates," my mom says.

"Yes, I am definitely one of the youngest graduates. I guess a lot of people join the FBI after they have done something else for a few years."

"See, you could have waited and joined the FBI later if you still thought you needed to," my mom scowls in her "I told you so" voice.

"We have been over this already, Mom. I have already done the hard part and graduated training. This is what I want to do."

"I know, honey, I just don't want you to get hurt. We are proud of you," my mom admits.

"You said you had all the stuff out of your apartment moved into storage right?" my mom confirms.

"Yes, it was done by movers right after I left," I reply hoping Agent Smith had it done.

"Well I was driving by there the other day and the floor you lived on had a fire. They have to gut and redo it. I'm glad you got all your belongings out of there first," my mom says, relived.

I wonder if Agent Smith was involved in the fire. I hope it was not Lilly and Tina. It was probably just an accident. Not every bad thing has to be related to me.

My parents stay for a while longer then head to their hotel. It was good to see them but I don't like deceiving them. I know if I told them the truth, they would freak, so I don't have any choice. Agent Smith was right about this job making it hard to deal with friends and family. If I had a regular job and moved far away from them I guess it wouldn't be a lot different. I wouldn't see them much then either but I would have to lie less.

I receive a package with my next assignment information. The package also contains detailed instructions on a location to go for a meeting. There are also keys and a map to the location of a car parked in the Quantico lot for me.

I'm next assigned, to report to the Armed Forces Experimental Training Activity (AFETA) facility run under the auspices of the Department of Defense

(DoD). This facility is called Camp Peary, a military reservation in York County, near Williamsburg, Virginia. I'm told it is known as "the farm" within the intelligence community.

I follow the instructions and go to the car left for me and head towards the meeting place. The location is down a gravel road about an hour from Quantico, out in the middle of nowhere. I'm supposed to arrive at 1p.m. When I get there, I see an old abandoned two-story house with an attached garage. I pull up and go in with my weapon drawn. After a couple minutes of looking around the house Agent Price steps out where I can see him.

"Good to see you made it through FBI training. I have been asked to give you a package. I don't know what is in it and I don't want to know. You are involved in some stuff way above my pay grade. Here is the package," Agent Price says, tossing me a sealed box just bigger than briefcase size.

"Thanks. It's good to see you, too," I reply not really knowing what to say.

"Since I dropped you off at Quantico five months ago, I have been doing menial work for the agency. Then out of nowhere, I'm assigned to bring this package here. I ran all over four states in the last twenty-four hours with this package. I changed cars five times and even took a short plane ride. I also had to check in every six hours. I'm pretty sure no one could have followed me. Well, good luck with whatever you are doing. My mission is over so until next time, see ya," Agent Price offers as he walks out to the house to get his car.

I take the package back to my car and drive off. I go to the parking lot of a supermarket I saw on the way here. Then in the midst of lots of cars, I park, lock the doors and open the package. Inside the package is a briefcase.

I use my gift to concentrate on the briefcase. I see a vision of the briefcase being made. I see a vision of the briefcase being purchased. I see a vision of Agent Smith putting items in the briefcase. The briefcase has no emotional attachment to anyone who affected it because of the short emotionless visions I get from it.

The briefcase is locked with two heavy-duty combo locks. A post-it note is stuck to the briefcase.

"The month and day when you first met old friends?" the note reads.

I enter in 0529 as the combination for May 29th the night I spent at the Goodrest Ranch. The briefcase pops open and I look inside. There is a note of instructions, a passport, and a driver's license all with my picture but the name Bianca Rizzoli. Bianca is an Italian American assigned to go through training at the Armed Forces Experimental Training Activity (AFETA) facility. Bianca is obviously going to be one of my aliases. I read the note of instructions.

"Go to Williamsburg First Savings Union and get a safety deposit box under your name. Place all your

personal identification in the safety deposit box including your FBI badge. Then you are to become Bianca Rizzoli, see enclosed dossier. If someone asks you a personal question, just do not answer, or ask them one in return. No one knows Bianca Rizzoli so do not worry about being caught in lies, but it is often best not to speak at all about personal things. Proceed to your next assignment until reassigned. Upon being reassigned come back to the bank and switch identification back to your real name. Once this is done call me. Burn this note after reading it. Good luck. S." the typed note reads.

I figure "S" stands for Agent Smith. I read over the note a couple times then burn it. I read through Bianca Rizzoli's information to get my head around it. There is very little there so I figure that is all I will need to know. I don't think we are going to be sharing our life story with other spies. I just need enough to get me by and say no comment on the rest. Bianca does speak Italian, but so do I, so no problem there.

I do as I'm instructed and get the safety deposit box. I leave all my identifiable items in it including the dossier on Bianca Rizzoli, my FBI badge and issued handgun. Once I leave the bank, I feel naked. If I was hit by a car and killed, I would be identified as Bianca Rizzoli. It is strange becoming someone else, even if that person does not exist.

I pull up to the gate of "the farm" about dusk. I'm on the list and get sent right on through. I'm assigned a room and get settled. The next day classes start.

I'm attached to a class going through Special Operations Group (SOG) training. SOG is a part of the Special Activities Division (SAD) of the CIA. SOG is responsible for covert operations, black operations and paramilitary operations. SOG functions and is organized like a professional military force, but does not have official military status. SOG conducts operations including high threat military or intelligence operations with which the U.S. government does not wish to be overtly associated. They also collect information in hostile countries and regions around the world. SOG teams are often six members who work as a unit and are not allowed to carry any objects or clothing that would associate them with the United States government. If they are caught, the U.S. government will deny any association to them.

I'm attached to the SOG team, under the cover story of being an alternate in case one of them becomes unable to perform their duties when they are deployed in the field. The team is made up of Dwight, Judith, Doug, Pam, Glen, and Bob. We do not use our last names with each other. I assume the less we know about each other's true identity the better. The names they are using may not be real, just like my name Bianca is an alias.

Dwight appears to be the leader of the group. He is around thirty and not bad looking. He seems to be a general jack-of-all-trades. Judith is in her mid-thirties and the prettier of the two women. She is a bully who tries to put other people down to make her look bigger. She is best at working people for information. Doug is in his late twenties and a little better looking than Dwight. He is the main tech person of the group. Pam is in her mid-twenties and above average looking. She is good at being a thief and specializes in getting around security systems. Glen is the best looking of the guys and the face man of the group. He works all their female contacts. Bob is small and skinny. He looks kind of like a serial killer. He is best at killing people, especially up close with knives. Bob is the one I would least like to be cornered by and the one I avoid the most.

On the first day of class, I meet these other members of my SOG team. Our instructor takes me to the room where we are meeting for the day. He stands in front of the others and introduces me.

"This is Bianca. She will be going through this training with you. She is now a full member of the team in all respects, so treat her as such," says Clark, our instructor for this part of the training.

I can tell by the icy stares that I'm not going to be accepted that easily. They were a team of six who all knew each other and I am the outsider. The women seem to be the ones most annoyed. They probably feel

I'm the biggest threat to them since I could take their place on the team. Well, I'm here to learn and leave, but they do not know that and I can't tell them.

"Welcome aboard," Dwight says.

"Thanks," I smile as I take a seat with the rest of the team.

"Aren't you a little young for this sort of work?" Judith accuses, looking me over.

"I made it here, didn't I?" I respond.

"Bianca, what kind of name is that anyway?" Judith smirks.

"I figure all your many years of experience would let you know things like that already. Did you come here to train, or just move your mouth all day?" I jab knowing Judith is trying to bait me into a fight.

"Give it a rest, Judith. Let's just get to work," Doug says.

Judith is pissed but she drops it for now. Clark starts the class and everyone becomes more professional. Clark goes over tons of different weapons. We have real examples of all the weapons and their ammo. I am amazed at all the different kinds of guns and ammo. I would think that guns would be more standardized in what kind of ammo they use, and I guess that is the current trend but there are still a lot of different kinds of ammo out there. We are looking at guns from all over the world. In the FBI training, we touched on this but concentrated on the few weapons that are commonly found within the U.S. In this class, we are looking at everything. Over a period of weeks, we get to fire many of the weapons. We are also made to field strip several of the common guns and learn to put them back together. We even have a few we have to learn to assemble in a pitch-black room so we cannot see what we are doing. I know less than the others about these weapons but I'm still very good at the putting them back together part.

We learn to shoot under different light and weather conditions. They put us in special areas that simulate dark rooms, twilight, sunrise, high noon sun and sun in your eyes. There are also weather rooms and corridors where I get drenched with rain-like water as I am made to shoot moving targets. I also go through the shooting range in snow, high winds, and rain and high wind together.

We do an extensive course in hand to hand fighting. I learn much more than I did in the FBI training. We learn to fight with objects of opportunity as well as knives and batons. A lot of the combat focuses on disabling and killing blows. My martial arts background serves me well and I become top of the class with Bob running a close second.

We learn to make bombs out of C-4, as well as common items like chemicals and fertilizer. We learn how to add devices like timers, remote detonators and motion sensors to bombs. We, then, detonate these bombs to have firsthand experience with them. We also learn to disarm bombs. I know I could not disarm a complicated bomb, but a basic one, like the ones I learn to make, I can disarm.

We have to complete the Countering Terrorist Tactics Course (CTTC) for driving several different times under different circumstances like with other drivers, chases, rain, sleet, ice, high random winds, controlled spins, high-speed turnarounds, precision stopping, running blockades, while being shot at, fending off attacks and with a flat tire. We even learn how to steal cars, get around their security systems and hot wire vehicles. This gives us real world experience and makes me more confident driving a car. I really enjoyed this part of the training. It is like being in a super powered bumper car. It is scary as hell, but I am really good at it. My danger sense gives me a huge edge over the rest of the team.

I never knew but a lot of the CIA work is about what is called Human Intelligence (HUMINT). HUMINT is intelligence gathering by means of interpersonal contact. HUMINT is defined as a category of intelligence derived from information collected and provided by human sources. In this training, we learn about conducting interrogations and having conversations with people having access to pertinent information. We learn to spot, assess, develop and recruit potential people who we can gain information from. We are trained to look at everyone we meet to spot if they could be useful to our organization as a source of valuable information. Once we identify a potential person we have to assess if they truly are in a position to have access to valuable information and if they would likely spy for us. Next, we develop a relationship with the person. We show interest in things they like, we flatter, schmooze and generally lie to get them to become our "friends." All the while, we are dropping very subtle hints that we may be more than we say and that we like them for their information as much as for themselves. Then, finally, we recruit them. We actually tell them what we have been hinting at for some time now that we want them to provide us with information for something in return, usually money. This seems to be one of the most important things the CIA operative does. The Special Operations Group (SOG) team I am training with only does a quick refresher course on this that mainly focuses on interrogation and the less nice ways of getting information. Some types of torture are demonstrated as well as truth drugs.

We go on low-flight parachuting drops into hostile terrain and have to navigate to a specific spot. We land in woods, swamps, and water where we then have to travel several miles in a small amount of time. We did many of these jumps alone so we could not rely on other team members. I enjoyed the flying through the air part but the hard landing sucked.

We learn how to trail people on foot and while in a vehicle. How to use tracking devices and bugs. I learn how to know if I am being followed and how to lose a tail. How to detect bugs and their best placement within different types of rooms and objects. We also learn how to bypass locks and security systems.

The FBI training was all by the book. This training is more about stomping on the book, rubbing it in the dirt, and then throwing it out the window. I know most of the things we are learning are against the law but these operatives are supposed to be working outside the U.S. on covert operations. When your life depends on the outcome of your mission, I guess the rules do not apply. We actually do everything hands on and in as real conditions as possible. I am tired and drained every night.

At the end of sixteen hard weeks of training, I am reassigned and leave "the farm". I make sure I'm not followed and go to Williamsburg First Savings Union to my safety deposit box. I put in all my Bianca identification and retrieve my real identification. I next call Agent Smith.

"Hello, Agent Smith, that was some very interesting training you sent me to."

"I hope you enjoyed it. I see that you scored very well in all areas. The more real world training you receive should serve you well. It is now time for you to report to your duty station and to your PR job. The information about the PR job was in the briefcase you received before. I have arranged for a note in your file giving you the right to carry a gun at all times, even though you just work in public relations. I assume you still want to join our organization."

"Yes. I think I will be bored by a normal life now. I have seen too many of the other possibilities."

"Ok. I will contact you in the next six months. Do a good job in your PR position but try not to call too much attention to yourself," Agent Smith challenges, then the line goes dead.

Chapter Six:
Falling

Two days later, I report to my duty station at the Kansas City, Missouri, field office of the FBI. I am to be the Kansas City Media Coordinator for the FBI. My title is Public Affairs Specialist Rebecca Shaw. Everything that goes out to the public or press concerning our office goes through my desk.

I'm surprised at how normal the job is. Sure, some of the subject matter is a little strange, being about criminal activities, but it is really an office job. I do have to make some face time with the brass in my office and with the press and public, but I would have to do that working for any company.

I get a furnished apartment and try to settle in. Kansas City is not Seattle, but it is a nice town. It has less traffic than Seattle and is much more spread out. The FBI office building is located on the outskirts of downtown. There are two small trendy areas nearby called Westport and the Plaza. The Plaza is more upscale and high-end. Westport is more artsy and eclectic.

My apartment is just off the Plaza. It is close enough that I can walk to many places to shop and eat. After the first week, I'm feeling pretty good about things. The job is going well and I love my new place and the area. I hit some nightlife and check out the local club scene. I meet a guy named Brian at a Westport club and we hit it off. We dance the night away and I give him my number. Two days later Brian calls me.

"Hi Becket. How've you been?" Brian asks.

"Doing well, just settling into the job and learning my way around the city. You?"

"The same old thing. I have been working on my house a little. I'm replacing most of the kitchen."

"Well, that should keep you pretty busy but it might be kind of hard to fix dinner," I offer helping Brian out a little.

"It does make cooking a challenge so I eat out a lot. Would you care to join me for dinner tomorrow night?" Brian asks, jumping on the opportunity I created.

"Sure we can do dinner. Do you want me to meet you or do you want to pick me up? I live down by the Plaza," I encourage knowing that at my place we can have some alone time to kiss before dinner.

"I can pick you up. Would around 7 o'clock be ok with you?"

I agree and give him my address. The next night Brian picks me up at my apartment. I choose a little white spring dress and sandals, as it is a particularly warm evening. I bring along a light sweater and a purse big enough to hold my gun just in case.

Brian is just a little older than I am. He has dark brown hair that is short and layered to one side. He has kind of a long face, which has a boyish charm to it. He is skinny but somewhat toned. Probably from all the biking he tells me he likes to do. He is around six feet tall and seems to always be smiling. His best feature is probably his butt, what little there is of it.

We go to dinner at one of the many Mediterranean cafes that dot the Plaza. We have a light dinner with some red wine. We chat and get to know each other better.

"I'm in public relations with the local branch of our company," I relate, taking a sip of my wine.

"I can tell you are good at your job because you answered my question but said nothing," Brian smiles at me.

"Saying I do PR work is easier than explaining who I work for. I could tell you but then I might have to kill you," I laugh, half joking.

"Really, who do you work for?" Brian probes, obviously curious.

I open up my purse and making sure Brian does not see my gun, I pull out my badge and lay it in front of him. Brian smiles at me and looks at it suspiciously. He thinks it is fake until he picks it up and turns it over in his hand.

"Really? You work for the FBI? You have to be too young and, well, hot to work for the FBI," Brian says amazed, still holding my badge.

"Well, thanks, I think, but I do work for the FBI. I do PR work for them, but I'm a full agent."

94

"Like with a gun and everything?" Brian wonders, seeming to look at me wondering where I would carry one.

"I work in public relations. Sure I have a gun, but am not called to use it in my day to day job," I defend, starting to feel a little self-conscious.

"Do you have a gun now? On our date?"

"Yes. Is that a problem? I'm trained and licensed to carry it," I snap, feeling like I'm being attacked.

"That's pretty cool. I never knew any woman who had her own gun or worked in law enforcement before," Brian confesses, handing my badge back. "I feel kind of boring now. I just work in computer networking."

Brian drops the conversation about my job, which I am grateful for. We sit and drink wine still getting acquainted. I don't talk much about myself. When the questions turn back to me I deflect by asking questions about the area or his background.

Over the next couple of weeks, I see Brian often and we become lovers. He pries about my work and past from time to time but I deflect the conversations. I know he wants to get closer to me. I do like him but I know I'm going to move on anytime now. I don't want either of us to get hurt. I just want to enjoy something normal in my life.

****

Three months into my post at Kansas City, I'm getting pretty settled into my life. My nightmares have slacked off and I do not even think about Lilly and Tina every day. It has been over a year since my horror filled vacation at the Goodrest Ranch. I still carry a gun wherever I go and make sure to not be alone outside at night. I'm still seeing Brian but I think he wants more than I can give right now.

I meet Brian for dinner at a little Greek place we like down by Westport. We chat for a little while about our days and then the subject turns to my past.

"How are your parents doing?" Brian inquires.

"Fine. Do you want to see a movie later in the week?" I counter, trying to divert the conversation.

"You always do this. Why won't you talk to me about yourself?" Brian questions, looking me in the eyes.

"I need to keep a little distance," I admit, not liking the way Brian is looking at me.

"I feel just the opposite. I want to get closer. You should move in with me," Brian smiles, putting his hands around mine on the table.

"I don't think that is a good idea. I may be moving offices soon or having a lot more travel for work," I reveal, not wanting to hurt Brian.

"Maybe this, maybe that. Maybe I will have a car wreck but I still drive a car. I'm here now tonight. Live your life with me for the now. Come what may, I would like to be with you. I love you," Brian shocks me, looking deeply into my eyes.

He had to say it. He has been dancing around it for weeks but here and now he said the words he cannot take back "I love you." I was just trying to have a normal relationship with a normal guy and here it goes getting all complicated. How do I feel about him? Do I love him? I'm not really sure. I like him an awful lot but have been intentionally holding myself back. I can see that look in his eye. He is waiting for me to say it back. I'm running out of time to think.

"I don't know, Brian. Things are complicated in my life. I really do like you but I'm not ready to give you the commitment you deserve," I stammer because I don't really know what is right to say.

"Maybe your life would get less complicated if you shared it with someone. We all have emotional baggage we carry around but it gets a lot easier when you share the burden with someone you care about. I am willing to share your burden," Brian confesses and I know he really means it.

"I have much more baggage than you can imagine. You have no idea what you would be getting yourself into. I'm also not allowed to talk about the worst issues in my past because of my job," I admit, believing that to be mostly true.

"Share what you can and the rest I will accept on faith. I have been there in the night when you wake up in a cold sweat screaming from one of your nightmares. I have held you in the dark until you were calmed down enough to go back to sleep. I know you have been through some pretty bad stuff. I want to be with you no matter what emotional baggage you have," Brian pleads, as he squeezes my hands in his.

"Man, it is hard to scare you off," I tease, trying to lighten the mood a little.

"You are the best thing that has ever happened to me. I know that if I don't get you totally hooked on me, one day you will wake up and know you could do much better than me. So come on, baby, give me a little commitment, move in with me," Brian grins at me.

Brian is one of those nice guys who was always the friend and never the boyfriend. I usually go for the more bad boy types but Brian is more loving and real than any of them ever could be. I know he is a long haul guy who will stick with a relationship. I know I could kick his ass but with all my training, I could kick most Agent's asses. Oh, what the hell.

"I will take one drawer and a fourth of a closet. Take it or leave it," I smile back at Brian.

"Deal. We can start there," Brian agrees, leaning over the table and kissing me long and passionately.

I return Brian's kiss and feel good about life. Until recently with Brian, I had not felt hopeful about the future since before my visit to the Goodrest Ranch. Brian has been a big part of me getting my spirit back to where it used to be. I love his smile and I can feel the love within him for me. When we are together sometimes, he just looks at me and I can feel his love like a tangible thing wrapping around me. I guess I do love Brian. This has just gotten a whole lot more complicated.

Over the next month, I start to use the "love" word back to Brian when he says it. I have also pretty much moved in with him. I have not moved that much of my stuff or given notice on my lease but I spend most every night at Brian's house.

I'm in the part of a relationship I call the fall. As in, I am falling in love. This is the beginning time when neither partner has really hurt the other much, when I feel more and more connected and trusting of Brian. We are falling together holding on to each other for dear love. We hope and pray that our partner has the strength of love to keep us up in the air and not let us go splat on the hard surface of reality that we try not to look at below. In a perfect relationship, my partner would be able to keep me falling in their love forever. In a great relationship, my partner will be able to get me airborne again even after I go splat face first into the hard harsh reality of love so I can fall in their love once again.

I tell Brian my idea about love and he likes it. We then start telling each other "I fall you" sometimes, instead of I love you. Brian sure makes me feel like he can keep me flying on his love for a long time.

One Friday night, we dance at a club until closing and walk through Westport afterwards. I would have never done this sort of thing even two months ago. I'm usually so careful to keep to high traffic or well-lit areas. I also did not bring my gun tonight. I have been leaving my gun home a few times over the last month when we go places that I cannot really keep a close eye on my purse, like tonight when we went dancing. I do keep my expandable baton in my purse at all times.

This late at night there are almost no cars driving by and no pedestrians. We are alone with each other holding hands talking. We are just enjoying each other and the nice cool night. Being with Brian has made me more optimistic and I am trying to live in the now.

We turn down a small side street to head back to our car. The hair on the back my neck starts to stand up and I know we are in danger. I see movement in the shadows and I grab Brian's arm to stop him.

"What's wrong?" Brian worries, looking at my eyes that are darting all around.

"You do what I say. Whatever I say you do it! Understand?" I order quietly to Brian still holding firmly on to his arm.

"Is this role-play like when I was a pirate at home?" Brian teases playfully to me.

"No! Damn it, we are not alone. Get ready to do whatever I say. Get out your phone and call 911, NOW!" I demand, seeing more movement in the shadows.

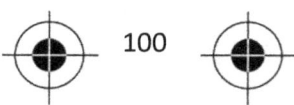

Brian fumbles with his phone. My hair is standing straight up and I know we could die where we stand. There is someone or something coming. God, what if it is Lilly and Tina. We are too exposed and I do not even have my gun. I will not leave home without it again. Damn me for thinking I could live a normal life.

We have to get to our car. I put my baton in my hand but do not expand it. Brian has dialed 911 and it is ringing. I grab Brian and pull him down the middle of the street toward our car. Just then, two young guys come out in front of us and there are two more behind us. Brian starts talking into the phone.

"We are in Westport and are being attacked by four men. We are just behind the Tornado club. Oh my god, they have knives," Brian murmurs as the men pull out knives.

"You're a pretty girlie. Pretty stupid to be out here so late. You can party with a real man now," offers the young tattooed man in front of us. I scan over his multiple piercings, greasy spiked hair and torn clothing before focusing on his darting eyes and shaking fingers. He is high, definitely an upper, probably meth. That makes him unpredictable, pain resistant and filled with a feeling that he can do anything.

"I'm a federal officer. You will leave this area or I will arrest you all," I vow much relived that it is not Lilly and Tina.

"That's funny," he laughs. "You look like you are still in high school, little one. Let's party!" he rushes us. He just made his first mistake.

"Don't run just stay behind me," I command Brian, keeping my eyes on the tattooed thug.

The thug flips his butterfly knife open and comes at me. He is more interested in scaring me than thinking I will put up a fight. I'm sure these guys want to rape me, but I have been trained to deal with scum like this. I'm a black belt and have had extensive hand-to-hand fighting training by the government. These punks are in for a big surprise.

The tattooed thug comes right up to me with his knife hand extended out toward me. That was his second mistake. I flip the baton to its full sixteen-inch extended length as I bring my arm up and down in one fluid motion. My baton cracks down on the thug's wrist and I can hear the bones break.

"Ahhh…you damn, bitch. You broke my damn hand. Get her," he yells as his knife falls to the ground and he drops to his knees from the pain.

"Federal agent! You are all under arrest," I order, turning on the next thug that is coming at us.

"No, we can't run they are all around us. We are being attacked. My girlfriend is an FBI agent and she is fighting them," I hear Brian muttering into the phone to the police.

The other one from the front rushes in with an illegal length switchblade his eyes wild. He thrusts his

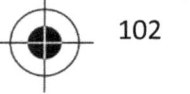

blade at me and I leap back. I bring my baton down and catch him in the shoulder. He moves back and tries to figure out his next move.

The two from the back have closed in and I push Brian back so all three are in my front view. They look at each other and start moving together. The hair on the back of my neck stands straight up giving me the second I need to anticipate their attack.

The one in the middle moves first. He is wearing a black baseball cap and holding a butterfly knife. He slices at me but lunges too far putting himself off balance. I move to the left and bring my baton down on his shoulder. He falls to the ground but not completely knocked out. The one to the left takes a swing at me with his knife since I sidestepped towards him to get out of the way of the last attack. My danger sense warns me and I parry his blow with my baton. He recovers quickly and presses his attack. The one from the right charges in also. They both come at me and I side step, while bringing my baton down on the one to the right's arm breaking it. He crumples onto the street in pain.

The one to the left is the only one that has not been hurt. He looks at his fallen comrades and looks like he is going to run. I attack him savagely and break his spirit quickly with a few quick blows. He falls to the ground, the fight all out of him. I kick the knives away from the men towards where Brian is standing. Brian starts to pick up a knife but I stop him.

"Those are evidence, don't touch them," I warn as we start to hear sirens in the distance.

I continually walk around the group of four men to make sure they don't try to run.

"You are all under arrest. Put your hands behind your head and lay flat on the street face down," I order the thugs.

I read them their rights and continue to watch them. Brian is kind of in shock. I take the still open cell phone from him and talk into it.

"This is Agent Shaw of the FBI. I have contained the situation. There are four assailants that need medical attention. They assaulted my friend and me after I identified myself as a federal agent. We can hear the police and will remain on scene to help with the report," I say into the phone still walking around the men on the ground.

I see a movement in an alley off to the side. My eye goes to the movement and I see a grizzly old man in overalls step out of the shadows and look at me. Our eyes lock and I know I have seen him before. Then I see him scoop a peach slice out of a can with a wicked looking claw can opener and stick it in his mouth. I watch as he chews the peach with what few teeth he has. Corky from Goodrest Ranch has returned.

One of the thugs tries to get away, but I kick him back to the ground. I look back at the alley but Corky is gone. I wonder if he was behind the thugs attack on Brian and me.

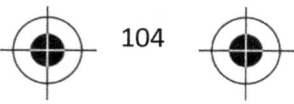

The police arrive and I show them my badge and give a statement. The men who attacked us are taken away. We are released to go home. Brian has to give a statement to the police, still in a little shock from the whole thing.

We go home to Brian's house. Brian does not talk about what happened at all. He doesn't really talk to me about anything and we just go to bed.

The next day we sleep late. Brian is awake when I get up and I sense that the questions are going to start. He has a distant look in his eye and I know I am in danger of losing his loving support and falling flat on my face. I have to be careful here or our relationship could be over.

"How did you know those guys were there last night? I had no idea," Brian questions' sitting at the far end of the couch away from me.

"I have been trained to notice things."

"I have never seen anyone so calm when fighting. You were not afraid of them at all," Brian accuses, looking at me as if I am a strange creature he is seeing for the first time.

"Again, I have been trained. I was fearful of my life and yours, but I had no choice but to fight. They would have raped me and probably killed you. I did what I was trained to do," I defend.

"I'm not sorry you stepped in and fought them off. I'm just surprised at how calm and efficient you were at it. Are all FBI agents that way?"

"Most FBI agents investigate after the fact. I'm sure they get lax as time goes by and out of practice in hand to hand fighting. You know I go to martial arts class twice a week and work out at the gym. I have just recently come out of training so offensive and defensive attacks are all fresh to me. I have also, sad to say, been in a much worse situation than we were in last night," I confess, trying to make Brian understand.

"You were something else last night. I will remember that the rest of my life. I feel a little inadequate around your bad self," he laughs jokingly.

I know the crisis is over. Brian has always thought it was cool I was in the FBI. He just has come to realize I can kick serious butt too. He will hold on to that image of me and be happy.

Chapter Seven:
Brian

It has been five months now and still no call from Agent Smith. I try to pull back from Brian a little but it is no use. I am in fall with him and he loves me. We are good together and I'm happy. Brian talks about the future sometimes and I'm even starting to believe there could be a future for us. We finish up work on his kitchen and his little house really starts to feel like a home. I know I'm getting too comfortable in this normal life. I take out the phone Agent Smith gave me and just stare at it wondering if it will ever ring. I'm not even sure I want it to ring anymore. Agent Smith said I had until I entered into his organization to decide. I could still turn back and just keep my life here with Brian. But what if Lilly and Tina show up one day? Could I live with Brian being hurt? We could both die. Brian would say I should not live in the "what ifs", just live in the now, take a risk and hope bad things will not come. I haven't had a nightmare in two months, I know it is because of my secure relationship with Brian.

My parents are coming for a visit to meet the man I have been telling them about on the phone and in emails. I think my mom is more excited than I am about Brian. She is so happy for me. I pick them up at the airport and get them settled in their hotel. We are all having dinner together so they can meet Brian. We go to a nice Italian place.

My mother starts talking to the waiter in Italian, telling him how we want our food cooked. I know Brian does not want his as spicy as she is saying so I interrupt and correct her in Italian. Brian looks at me and I know I'm in trouble.

"So you speak Italian?" Brian accuses, looking at me.

"She can speak five languages and also read Latin," my mom praises, before I can answer.

"I had no idea," Brian confesses, looking from me to my mom. I can see that he has an evil idea to get information out of my mom about my past.

"What languages?" Brian probes my mom.

"Rebecca speaks Italian, Friulian, Slovene, and German, oh, and English," my mom clarifies obviously enjoying talking to Brian.

"I have never heard of Friulian or Slovene before, where are they from?" Brian inquires.

"My family is from a northern area of Italy called Carnia. Friulian is one of the old languages of Carnia. Slovene is spoken in Slovenia which used to be part of Yugoslavia until it became its own country," my mother relates, enjoying talking about the old countries of her childhood.

"Was Becket born in Carnia?" Brian stammers, butchering the accent.

"Oh no, she was born in the U.S. but I was born and raised in Italy. Rebecca used to spend every summer and Christmas in Italy," my mom says proudly.

I sit there watching my mother and Brian talking about my past and feel kind of helpless to stop it. I guess there is not much harm in it but I should be the one to reveal these things, not my mother. I can see my dad watching me squirm in my chair. He is amused by the show.

"Did you stay in Carnia when you went to Italy?" Brian asks.

"We did travel sometimes, but it was mostly in Carnia in the valley of Degano. Degano is my maiden name. Our family is very prominent in that part of the world," my mother smiles even more proudly.

"I had no idea. That is so very interesting," Brian admits, looking at me.

"I was surprised to find out that Becket works for the FBI but she never told me why she joined," Brian says.

"Mother, please!" I plead trying to get her to stop.

"He has a right to know if you two are going to have a lasting future. Do you intend to have a long lasting future with my daughter?" my mom interrogates Brian.

"Yes, I intend that very much," Brian agrees very sincerely.

"I see what you mean Rebecca, he is very much in love with you," my mom says, patting Brian's hand on the table.

"Rebecca went on a vacation to a horse ranch. There were several murders the night all the guests arrived and only Rebecca made it out alive. Shortly after that, she met a man who was in the FBI. I guess he talked her into joining. She said she wanted the training to make her feel safer," my mom exposes looking at me sadly.

"Oh my god. Is that why you have nightmares? I had no idea. Well, Mrs. Shaw, I would not worry about Rebecca. She can take care of herself. I have seen that first hand," Brian promises looking from me to my mom.

"Do you still have those nightmares, honey? Wait, you have seen her fight?" my mom demands.

I try to wave Brian off but he does not notice.

"Oh yeah, she fought these four muggers one night when we were out late and walking back to our car. They all had knives. She beat them all down and arrested them. It was amazing," Brian spouts realizing too late he is talking to my worrying mom.

"Rebecca Nicola! You did not tell me you were in a knife fight. You could have been killed," my mom accuses shaking her finger at me.

I can see Brian has lost his nerve to talk for a minute so I jump in.

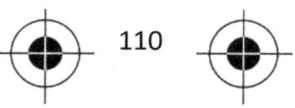

"I didn't want to worry you. As Brian said, I had the situation well in hand. If I had not been trained I might be dead so you should be happy I joined the FBI," I say, standing up for myself.

"I just worry about you. I'm glad you know how to take care of yourself," my mom sighs.

"How is your job going?" my dad interjects, changing the subject for me.

"It is going well. I'm really starting to understand what I need to do on a day-to-day basis. I am good at my job so that helps," I say, looking at my dad thankfully for changing the subject.

"You always avoid this question on the phone so I am going to ask it in person. Where were you for the sixteen weeks after FBI graduation?" my mom asks, going back to things I don't want to talk about.

"I was in training. I have told you that," I restate.

"I had your father look into it and there is no record of you training with the FBI during that time," my mom accuses.

I look at my father like "what the hell" and he just shrugs his shoulders and looks at the ground. He's not going to be any help. I look at Brian and can tell he wants to know as much as my mom.

"I was in training. That is all I can say. You can believe me or not," I offer.

Mom and Brian are disappointed in not getting more, but they both love and believe me.

"Your father also looked into that Agent Weis that you brought to the house before you went off to FBI school. He found out he died the same night we met him. His body was found in the parking lot of your apartment building in Seattle. Then your apartment burns up a few days later. What is that all about?" my mom demands, giving me her worst "mom" look.

I feel trapped. I had no idea dad would use his connections to check up on me. What should I tell them? All three of them are staring at me now.

"First you can't repeat any of this to anyone. Not a priest or family member, anyone. Agreed?" I insist.

They all agree.

"Agent Weis was not my boyfriend. He was assigned with another agent to protect me. It was believed that the person who committed the murders at the Goodrest Ranch might be after me. I joined the FBI so I would be prepared in case they ever came after me. The night Agent Weis died, he was protecting me from the ones who committed all those murders at the Goodrest Ranch. I and the other agent barely escaped with our lives," I relate, remembering seeing Agent Weis die.

They all look at me with open mouths. I have stumped even my mother who loves to hear herself talk.

"The sixteen weeks after FBI training I was going through advance training of a field agent so I would be prepared to deal with a potential murderer stalking me," I clarify.

They are even more stunned by this.

"I have been trying to keep my distance from you, Brian, because I don't know if I'm still a target. The FBI seems to think I am. I don't want you to get hurt," I confess looking at Brian.

"You have been carrying a lot on your shoulders, little girl. We will do what we can to help you," my dad reassures.

"The thing is you can't really help me. I have trained myself about as well as I can. I watch the shadows and am vigilant against possible danger. I love you all but you are untrained, and are a way someone could use to get to me. I joined the FBI to learn how to protect myself but also to create a little distance between us, Mom and Dad, so you would not be targets. I know you don't know this but the FBI watched your house for a month after the death of Agent Weis to keep you safe," I admit looking at my parents.

"Brian, I know you say live in the now and do not worry about maybe or what ifs but my what ifs could end in your death. I couldn't bear that. I wish you would have just let me deal with this myself and not pushed me to tell you. Now nothing will ever be the same between us. I am sorry," I mutter, as I get up and walk out of the restaurant.

Brian tries to follow me but I know how to disappear and he never sees me. He soon goes back in to be with my parents.

I wander the streets alone after dark. I know I should get where there are more people but I do not care right now. I don't know what to do. I have messed up everything with the people I love. My parents and Brian will always wonder if a mass murderer is coming to get them as long as they are near me. Damn it, I could have maybe married Brian and even had kids. My mom says you always have to be truthful with the ones you love, but she didn't tell dad about my gift for years, and she kept my being in a coma from him for three weeks. I think it would have been better if they never knew I'm being hunted by a mass murderer. The funny thing is no matter how bad they think it is it is way worse. I'm hunted by at least two vampires who will never age and probably never forget me. They could come for me tonight or when I'm sixty and be just as deadly either time.

I take out the phone Agent Smith gave me. Is this the right decision? Brian will never look at me the same way again. It is time to join with Agent Smith and start my future. I push the speed dial for Agent Smith and it starts ringing.

"Yes," the voice on the phone says.

"Agent Smith?" I ask to make sure.

"Yes, Becket it is me. Are you alright?" Agent Smith inquires.

"Not really. I think I am ready to join your organization," I hesitate, not as sure as I thought I was.

"I was going to call you in a couple of days anyway. There will be a window for you to come to us in a week. Next Friday you will need to get in your car packed for a long vacation. Travel south down 71 hwy towards Joplin, MO. I will call you at 8pm that night. Be close to Joplin by then."

"What will they think happened to me at work?"

"You are going to be lent out to a company that works with the FBI for an extended period. You will still be on the books in the Kansas City office but working elsewhere," Agent Smith clarifies.

"Ok, I'll be waiting for you call," I say, hoping the week goes by fast.

"Talk to you on Friday," Agent Smith adds hanging up.

Just one more week, I can make it one more week. I will have to tell Brian and my parents but not tonight. Tonight I'm going to a hotel to be alone. My sleep is plagued with nightmares of Lilly and Tina savaging Brian and my parents with their vampire fangs. The smell of their blood and the horrible sounds of their screams haunt me. The dream ends with me being drown in their blood as I try to save them.

The next night I arrange to see Brian and then see my parents after. I meet Brian at a pub for drinks to talk. I probably should go somewhere more private with him but I'm not that brave right now.

"I'm sorry I ran out on you last night. I needed time to think," I confess, feeling somewhat bad for sticking Brian with my parents.

"It is ok, Becket. I talked to your parents a lot last night after you left. I know you used to have nightmares all the time and they went away when you were with me. I cannot protect you or myself from who might be coming for you. I know that," Brian admits, taking my hand in his. "But I can ease your mind and make you happy. I know death could come at any time from a car wreck or from something related to your job or past. But I want to spend every moment of the life I have with you." Brian vows looking at me while he gets on one knee and takes out a ring.

"Will you do me the extreme honor of becoming my wife?" Brian hopes, slipping a very nice ring on my finger.

I look down at the ring. It is a round cut center diamond with deep blue sapphires on either side. I know it's blue because Brian's favorite color is blue. The band is gold.

What the hell do I do now? I bet he asked my parent's permission and they are in on this. My telling Brian that I was hunted by a mass murderer did not

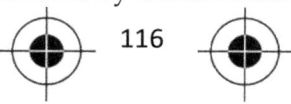

put him off. I was prepared to go splat from my falling in love with Brian. Nevertheless, he surprised me again and his love has kept me aloft and still falling in love with him. In six days, I'm supposed to meet Agent Smith and begin my new life in his organization. How can I marry Brian? I don't know what to say. Brian looks up at me and I can see he expects an answer. People in the pub are looking at us as well and all wanting an answer. But I don't know the answer.

"I'm not sure Brian. I am so sorry. I'm really confused right now with what to do with my life. I love you. I fall you. But my life is even more complicated than you know. Let me wear the ring and think about it. Is that ok?" I plead, pulling Brian off the floor to sit next to me.

"Yes, Becket, I will give you time. I love you so much. As long as we love each other it will be ok," Brian reassures before kissing me.

I can feel his love for me flowing into me. His love envelopes me and I am powerless against it. If he asked me to marry him at this moment, I would have to say yes.

"What else is going on in your life?" Brian probes.

"What I told you was all true but I left certain things out. I was recruited by the FBI to help capture the mass murderer who I encountered at the Goodrest Ranch. I have been trained far beyond what a normal agent gets. My job here in Kansas City is to establish a cover for when I go to work with this special task force. I have been notified that I am supposed to leave for the special taskforce on Friday and I have no idea when or even if I will be coming back," I reveal, searching Brian's eyes for his reaction.

"I could get in so much trouble for even telling you this. We could both go to jail over me even talking to you. I love you, and yes, in a normal world I would like to marry you, but I haven't lived in a normal world since that night at the Goodrest Ranch," I admit.

"Don't go. Stay here, work your PR job, and marry me. We could truly be happy," Brian begs, while he squeezes my hand in his.

"I don't think I can back out anymore. The date is set. You should leave me and find someone normal," I tell Brian.

"I like you, Becket, you have become my best friend. I love you, Becket, and I don't want to lose you. I don't want someone normal, I want you. You know I love that you work for the FBI. I even think it's cool you're a bad ass in a fight. I don't want you going away from me on secret missions but if that's the only way I can have you then that's what I'll take," Brian vows, looking into my eyes to show me he really means it.

"I don't think you know what you are saying. I might be gone weeks or months at a time and not even able to contact you. You could never tell anyone what I really do, ever. Do you really want to live that lie? I have been doing it, and it's not fun at all," I confess.

"I think I could do it. You are one of the good guys, right? I'm proud of that. We could make it work," Brian hopes.

"I will think about it. You cannot tell any of this to my parents. Do you understand?"

"Yes, I understand. Speaking of your parents, they should be waiting for us at the restaurant. What do you want to tell them about the ring?"

"I figure you already told them you were going to ask me, right?"

"Yes, late last night I asked your father for his permission to marry you. They know I was going to ask you tonight," Brian admits, looking as if I caught him doing something bad.

"I love that you asked my dad first, Brian. Let's tell them we are engaged but we are not going to rush in to anything, so haven't set a date yet."

"That sounds pretty much like the truth," Brian smiles at me.

Oh boy, I am in trouble with this one. He is going to keep that ring on my finger any way he can. Not that I mind that much. It fits my finger quite well. The problem is I could get real used to wearing this ring.

Over the next week, I make arrangements to go away for an extended period of time. I make sure Brian understands that he cannot call my office looking for me or even my cell. I will contact him and it could be up to a year. I know the thought of a year really freaks him out but I want him prepared. I also tell him that I may contact my parents and not him if I only get one call. I make sure he knows it is not because I love him less but because my mother will force my father into trying to pull strings to find me and I cannot have that. I agree to be engaged to him but will not promise to marry him until we see how this new job and time apart affects us both.

When I depart, I leave my engagement ring with Brian as I know I would not be able to wear it. This upsets Brian a lot, but I would rather it be safe with him. We say our tear-filled goodbyes, and I head south to Joplin.

Chapter Eight:
Transition

At 8p.m., my phone rings and it is Agent Smith. "Are you near Joplin?" Agent Smith asks.

"Yes."

"Get off on 96 hwy and go into the town of Carthage."

"That exit is about five miles away."

"Good, get off the exit and take your third left. It will lead you to a storage facility called the Carthage Closet. Pull in and go to unit 103. There will be combo lock on it, which you know the combination to. Open it and put your car inside. Get your things and lock your car inside the garage. Then make your way down the lane to the opposite of where you drove in. There is a loose part of the fence you can slip through. I will meet you on the other side of the fence."

I do as I'm asked. I park my car, get my luggage and relock the garage. I make sure I'm not followed and make my way to the opening in the fence. Once through the fence, Agent Smith drives up in a car and I get in, putting my luggage in the back seat.

"Any problems?" Agent Smith asks as we drive.

"No, I did not see any tails and had no trouble finding this place," I report, checking the side mirror again just in case.

"Good."

We travel about fifteen minutes on small country roads. We pull down a dirt road and stop well out of sight of the blacktop we were on. Agent Smith gets out a bug detector and starts running it over me and then all my stuff. We get out of the car and he makes me open my suitcase and spread everything out so he can wand it better. After ten minutes of this using three different kinds of wands, we get back in the car and drive on.

"Sorry about that, but it is necessary. I need to take your cell also," Agent Smith apologizes.

"I understand. Someone could have slipped something in my stuff," I add, not really believing it myself.

Agent Smith is all business right now. I wonder if this is how he usually is? I think southern Missouri is a strange place to meet up. I figured the office I would be assigned to would be in a major city. But I don't know a lot about hunting the supernatural, yet.

We drive for an hour and I'm kind of lost. None of the roads down in this hilly Ozark area run in a straight line. We are constantly going up and down hills and following the curvy ridgelines. Most of the area is all overgrown forests with few houses. What towns I have seen have all been less than a thousand inhabitants and even a few having under a hundred.

We go down a gravel road that turns into a dirt road. We come up to a dilapidated house with an overgrown yard. There is a shed out back that Agent

122

Smith pulls the car into. By the amount of dust and cobwebs, I'm sure no one has been here in at least a year. Agent Smith hands me a flash light and gets one for himself.

"This is home for tonight," Agent Smith says getting out of the car and grabbing a bag from the trunk. He walks on toward the house, leaving me standing in the yard.

I get my bags and head through the tall weeds after Agent Smith. He goes around to the back of the house and uses a key to open the door. There is a chill wind in the air that creates a rustling sound as it travels through the trees. I will be glad to get inside the house and out of the dark night.

I'm surprised that the inside of the house is clean. Agent Smith shows me to a decent room with a single bed, desk and a single straight back chair. The best thing is the bathroom works.

It is around 10 p.m. by the time we get settled. I find Agent Smith at the kitchen table waiting for me. There is a stack of files in front of him. I sit across from him wondering what this is all about.

"I have some hard questions for you. We both need to make sure you are making the correct choice in joining our organization," Agent Smith announces.

"Ok, go ahead and ask," I say, squirming in my chair a little.

"Tell me about Brian."

"Brian is my boyfriend. We have been going out for five months. I did a security check on him after our second date. He looked clean."

"Are you planning to marry Brian?" Agent Smith probes as I wonder how he knows so much about my life.

"I don't know, maybe. He wants to marry me. I want to see if I can juggle a normal life and still be part of your organization before I make my decision," I admit.

"Do you love Brian?"

"Yes," I confess.

"If you were not joining my organization, would you be marring him?"

"Yes."

"Why did you not choose to be with him? Why are you here?"

"If I marry Brian, I want to know we are safe from Lilly and Tina first. I can't bear the idea of them coming and killing Brian," I admit.

"So you plan to kill Lilly and Tina and then run off and marry Brian, living happily ever after or some bullshit like that?" Agent Smith forces, pushing me to think things out.

"No. I'm not totally stupid. I know my chance of being happy with Brian or any semi-normal man is very slim. But I've tried to push Brian away several times and he just keeps loving me. He accepts whatever I tell him and keeps wanting to be with me.

I just want to have that in my life for as long as I can," I confess, welling up with emotion and trying to hold back the tears.

"What have you told Brian about our organization? He must know you are going to be gone for a long time," Agent Smith asks.

"I told him I could be gone up to a year and he could not try to find me. I told him about the Goodrest Ranch but left out the supernatural stuff. I led him to believe that I was recruited into the FBI to work with a special taskforce set up to capture the mass murderer that I encountered at the Goodrest Ranch. He knows it is top-secret stuff and cannot be revealed to anyone, even family. I have never spoken to him about the supernatural," I report looking at Agent Smith to try to gauge his reaction.

"He is ok with this scenario?"

"Kind of. He wants me to not join your organization and just keep my PR job with the FBI. He wants me to stay in Kansas City and marry him. However, he loves me as no one ever has before. He says he will take what of my time I can give him," I reveal, thinking about Brian and how much I already miss him.

"You know that even if you manage to somehow kill Lilly and Tina, you will not just be able to walk away from our organization. I don't think after all you will have been through that you could walk away even if you wanted to," Agent Smith warns.

"I understand that. I thought maybe I could spend my down time with Brian," I hope.

"What downtime? Who said there would be vacations?"

"You said this job is hard on the agents, so I figured we got time off to help deal with that," I hesitate.

"Very good, now you are starting to think. Yes, there will be down time between cases. It can be interrupted or canceled and often is"

"So I could see Brian during my off time?"

"Yes. However, you know the odds of you two having a successful relationship are very slim. You will never be able to tell him the full truth about your life."

"I understand and I think he does too. I know it may fall apart at any time. I'm surprised our relationship has lasted this long. But, being with Brian makes me happy and more grounded. When I was with him, my nightmares almost went away completely. It might be silly to hope for a husband and children someday, but I do," I confess, looking at Agent Smith curious about all the things he has given up for this job.

"So if you have to choose between Brian and this job, you choose the job? Is that correct?" Agent Smith forces.

"Yes, but I think I will be a better agent knowing I can go home to Brian every now and then," I say, hoping I didn't just completely give up Brian.

"Brian is an issue. We will wait and see how it plays out for now."

"Thank you, thank you very much," I say, meaning every word.

"Let's get some sleep. We will get an early start in the morning. Good night Becket," Agent Smith smiles as he walks to his room.

Chapter Nine:
HEL

The next morning, we drive deeper into the Ozark Mountains, which are really just big hills. The area we go to is even less inhabited. We are still traveling windy blacktop roads. After about an hour, we turn off onto a blacktop that is marked as a private road. After about a mile, I start seeing signs that are handmade and primitive looking.

"Private Property, Trespassers will be fed to the dogs!" the first sign reads.

"Hey stupid! Turn around or we will shoot you!" the next one reads.

"It's a long walk back. Turn back now or we will blow your tires," the next sign reads.

"Do you like the signs?" Agent Smith muses as he pushes something like a garage door opener and I see a tire puncture mat in front of us move off the road. We drive through, he pushes the button again, and the tire puncture mat resets.

"Ok, fool, it's killing time," this sign has a drawn picture of a person with a large hole in their head with blood dripping from it.

"The signs are not very government like. But I bet they are effective and are kind of funny," I admit.

"They are not supposed to be government. The locals think a survivalist group lives here. We encourage that idea. We control 100,000 acres all around here. Most of it is old-growth forest that has never been logged. We use it as a buffer to the Norms, what we call normal citizens," Agent Smith tells me.

We arrive at a high security gate and Agent Smith puts a key card in a slot. This activates an eye retina scanner. A voice sounds from of the control box.

"Identify please," the electronic voice says.

"Agent Smith and Agent Shaw," Agent Smith replies.

"Welcome to HEL, Agent Shaw," the voice out of the box squawks, kind of freaking me out.

"HEL, it is the acronym for our organization. Hunters of Eternal Lies or HEL for short. Somebody had to have had a sense of humor to come up with that one," Agent Smith chuckles to himself.

HEL, really? I guess most people think their work is HEL but mine really will be. What have I gotten myself into now?

After going through the gate checkpoint, we travel another five or six miles to another security checkpoint. The fences around this place are ten feet tall with razor wire on top. Agent Smith tells me they are electrified at kill levels. I have seen dozens of cameras along the road and at the checkpoint. These people are very serious about their privacy. Agent Smith has to use his key card, retinal scan and talk to the guard on the other end of the mic before we get through.

"Sat pass over in ten. Get under cover," the voice from the security box squawks.

Agent Smith drives faster than he has been through the checkpoint.

"What was that about?" I inquire.

"There is a satellite about to pass over the base. We need to get our car out of sight before it does," Agent Smith says.

We drive another couple of miles before we come to the first of the buildings. Most of the buildings are not large and are very close to trees. I am surprised that there are very few buildings in all. I am sure from above this place it would be hard to spot even from satellites. It would certainly look more like a survivalist camp than a government facility. It looks like the top of the buildings are made out of an unusual material. I've heard of experimental building materials that block sensory equipment and make the buildings look like natural ground clutter. I think that is what the roofs and walls of these buildings are made of.

We drive into a covered garage and park. The only vehicles in this whole place seem to be those in the garage. They must hide the vehicles inside these low imprint buildings so they are not detected. I wonder why HEL is worried about being spied on. Who would spy on the spies? Crazy alien fanatics, vampire wannabes, conspiracy theorists, other three letter agencies. I really wonder who they are hiding from.

We go to the far end of the garage and Agent Smith uses his keycard and retinal scan to access a heavy security door. The door leads to an elevator. We get in and I take note of the six buttons. From above, I would not believe there would be even one level below the almost undisturbed forest, let alone six.

Agent Smith has to use his key card, go through a retinal scan and talk to security again. I have to do the retinal scan as well. We then both must place our hand on a silver plate and push hard until a light turns green. A needle pricks our finger and takes a blood sample. Next, the elevator is flooded with light that is brighter than the sun for at least thirty seconds. I guess this simulates sunlight and is meant to hurt vampires. I can see that cameras in the elevator are monitoring all our actions. All this happens before the elevator will respond to the pushing of its buttons. The security in this place is incredible. I wonder if it is to prevent supernaturals or Norms from entering.

Agent Smith presses the first button on the elevator and the elevator moves down into the earth. Either the elevator is incredibly slow or the floor we go to is much further underground than a normal basement. The doors to the elevator open and we step out into an ultramodern facility. Everything is state of the art and pristine. We walk the halls seeing almost no one else.

"Wait here in the conference room. I will be back in a few minutes," Agent Smith orders as he walks off down the corridor.

A large oval table that appears to be a smart table that can bring up computer images dominates the conference room. The table has twelve chairs around it. There are several video screens along the wall as well as computer terminals. It looks like one of the long walls is one huge video screen.

The whole basement screams that it is a SCIF or sensitive compartmented information facility. SCIF's are totally secure from any kind of outside surveillance and have huge security. All the three-letter agencies have at least one SCIF. It seems to be kind of a penis envy thing among the top brass at the three-letter agencies to measure their worth by the size of their organization's SCIF. It looks to me that HEL has them all beat.

After a couple of minutes, Agent Smith returns with other people. Several come in the room and sit down. They all glance at me but go about their business. Agent Smith motions for me to sit down and he sits next to me. The Suit seated at the head of the table starts talking.

"Welcome Becket. I am Director Clayton Palmer. I run this facility. My staff and I wish to introduce ourselves and welcome you to Hunters of Eternal Lies or HEL for short. You will be known as Becket inside our facility. You will be assigned an alias to use in the field as necessary. You will go through some training here and be partnered with a senior Agent. When you are ready, you and your partner will be sent into the field to work cases," Palmer explains. Palmer is a handsome man in his early forties. He looks to be a suit, not a field agent. He has black hair cut in a conservative business style. His suit looks tailored and he looks at home in it.

"I am Assistant Director Kathy Carver," a very attractive woman in her early thirties scowls, staring at me in an examining way that I don't like at all. Carver has brown hair that she wears in a short layered cut. She is dressed in a light blue business suit. She seems cold and unapproachable.

"Hi, Becket, welcome aboard. I'm Frank Schroeder but please just call me Frank, everyone does. I'm head of research here at our underground HEL. If you need anything, feel free to ask. This place takes a little getting used to but it grows on you," a semi-balding man in his mid-thirties smiles at me. Frank is in a wheelchair that looks to be tricked out with all sorts of devices. He is certainly the most good natured of the staff so far.

"I am Field Supervisor Russell Hawkins. I will be in charge of your training here. It's good to have you on our team," a fairly handsome and clean cut man informs me. Hawkins looks to be in his late forties or maybe early fifties. He has short dark brown hair. He is more laid back than Palmer and dresses more for utility than style.

"Chad Easley, Head of Security here at HEL," a handsome man with a military bearing says giving me a head nod as a greeting. Easley is a good-looking guy in his late twenties. He has a military style hair cut for his brown hair. He is very well built and obviously keeps himself in top shape. He's about 5'9".

"We are the upper staff here. You will meet the others as you go. I will leave you in Agent Smith's care. I wish you well in your new life here," Palmer continues.

Agent Smith gets up and motions for me to do the same.

"It was nice to meet you all," I say as Agent Smith and I walk out of the conference room.

Agent Smith takes me to the dorm hall. My name is already on the nameplate of the door. My room is around twenty-five feet square. There is a single bed, a desk with a computer and chair, a nice lounge chair, a dresser, a small closet, two lamps and a tv screen that can be watched from the bed or chairs.

"This is home for now. Your luggage is being gone through and then will be delivered. Just standard procedure. Do you have any questions?" Agent Smith asks.

"Do you have any advice for me?" I probe, looking hopeful at Agent Smith.

"Study and pay attention. Learn what we have to teach you as well as you can, because it may save your life. Oh and try not to get on Carver's radar if you can help it," Agent Smith warns.

"Ok. What happens now?"

"You are the last new trainee to arrive. Your class is small. Get to know them. Tonight enjoy a meal in our fabulous cafeteria and get a good night's rest. The real HEL will start tomorrow in training," Agent Smith almost smiles at me.

"See you later," I wave as Agent Smith walks off down the hall.

I go through the drawers in my desk and find office supplies and notebooks. I look in the dresser and find several sets of camo-fatigues. I figure these are for training. The computer lets me log in but does not have any internet privileges. The screen on the wall has a selection of training videos accessible. I watch the first one since I have little else to do.

"Shape shifters," is the title of the video.

"Shape shifters are known to come in two types, the traditional werewolf form and that of animal forms. These two types seem to come from two completely different species."

"Werewolves have a human and a wolfman form."

The video shows a picture of a wolfman ripping through four police officers to get to an injured woman in a crashed car. The wolfman is shot at least six times before it rips the car door off its hinges and takes the unconscious women out of the car. The four police officers appear to have either been killed or very badly hurt. The wolfman is able to carry the injured woman away from the wreck even though it has multiple gunshot wounds.

"As you can see from this footage, werewolves are very real. This is one of the only known footage of a real werewolf."

"One of the policemen survived the attack. He was bitten and clawed in the attack. He was quarantined and watched for many months to see if he would turn into a werewolf. All blood work and testing showed no change in his anatomy. It is therefore believed that the bite and claws of a werewolf do not pass on the condition."

"We have reports that werewolves have an extreme allergy to silver. It burns them. This has not been confirmed but silver ammunition is available for requisition on a case by case basis."

"The video we have of the wolfman occurred at night but during a quarter moon so it is a myth that werewolves are only active during the full moon. The werewolf was after the woman in the car. From careful analysis of the video, it is believed that the werewolf was trying to help the injured woman. This would rule out the myth that werewolves are only beasts and monsters."

"The woman from the car was identified but has never been found. There have been some sightings of

her alive and well, but she has never been caught. She has been placed on the FBI's most wanted list as we want to question her about her connection to the werewolf."

"One of the werewolf's main abilities is instilling sheer terror in all who see them. Many witnesses are of little or no use in werewolf sightings. They seem to universally have a total blackout of the event or try to rationalize it away as a person in a mask or a dog attack. This has made it very difficult to get hard evidence about werewolves."

"There are very few cases of werewolf related fatalities. For this reason we believe that they are not an active threat to Norms."

"Besides silver the only other theorized weakness of a werewolf is fire. Traditional guns are not believed to be effective in killing werewolves but enough firepower might slow them down. These theories have yet to be tested."

"The other kind of shapeshifter is one that turns into animals. The animal shapes that have been reported are dog, cat, wolf and bat. We believe these shapes may be taken by vampires and have nothing to do with werewolves. We do not possess any video evidence of these abilities but there are a few credible eye witness accounts that make it necessary for us to be prepared for the possibility. There is an alternate theory in which these reports may be about animals who are themselves vampires. This is not widely believed and is not consistent with most of the eyewitness accounts but should be considered. It has been theorized that vampires in animal shapes would have a lower body temperature just like vampires in their human form. If this is the case, then thermal imaging should be able to detect a vampire in animal form."

There is a knock on my door so I turn off the video and answer it. A good-looking man in his late twenties is standing at my door. He has dark eyes and hair. His complexion looks Mediterranean. His dark hair is shoulder length and full of curls. I must say he looks pretty good to me and I can see by the way he is checking me out that he likes what he sees.

"Good evening, Becket. I am Renee LeClerc. It's my pleasure to escort you to dinner," the man winks with a heavy accent that I think is French.

"Good evening to you, LeClerc. Lead the way," I say, looking him over some more.

"This way, lovely lady," LeClerc offers me his arm.

I walk next to him but do not take his arm. He smiles at me with a look that says I had to try. I know LeClerc is going to be trouble. Brian is home waiting for me. I need to just focus on that. LeClerc takes me to the cafeteria. It is large enough to hold around fifty people, there are only six now including LeClerc and myself.

We order off a menu but place our order at a counter and have to pick up our food at another

counter. I bet the whole kitchen staff, including the counter, is only three or four people. The cafeteria is small and efficient. I order a chicken Caesar salad while LeClerc orders the t-bone and some pasta on the side. We go over and sit at a table with two other people sitting at it.

"This is Becket the last member of our class. Becket this is Dr. Brad Hasty and Lester Coontz," LeClerc smiles pointing at the men at the table.

"Nice to meet you, Becket. You can call me Brad. It's so nice to see someone of a more refined manner has finally joined our group. Between LeClerc's sports fanaticism or testosterone filled war stories and Lester's fits of horror filled flashbacks and guttural speak I was going insane. Please tell me you are more normal and ladylike," Brad begs, looking at me hopefully.

"I don't know about ladylike but I'm pretty normal. Pleased to meet you," I reply looking from Brad to Lester who seems to be staring into space lost in thought or maybe lack thereof.

"I was hoping for a nice strapping lad that would fall madly in love with me, but a pretty young girl will do. We can be the best of friends. LeClerc is nice to look at but I don't think I could ever really take him home to mom. He will be good for some sex but nothing long-term," Brad teases and I can see he is playing his being gay thing over the top to make LeClerc nervous.

"I look forward to it," is about all I can manage to say. LeClerc is pissed, but I can tell he has already had this fight with Brad a few times and lost, from the smile on Brad's face.

"Lester does not talk much when he's like this. He says he can see dead people. You know, like ghosts. I think he's best at butchering the English language myself," Brad continues.

"The Doc here is some kind of fancy blood Doc who works for the CDC. He thinks vampires are transmitting AIDS through their bites," LeClerc reveals looking skeptically at Brad.

"That's a simple way of explaining it, but yes, that is my theory. I was recruited for my expertise and ideas involving tracking vampires by their spread of AIDS," Brad admits.

"I'm here because I fought a vampire and lived through the experience," LeClerc announces proudly.

"I encountered a vampire that killed several people and survived. I'm here because of that experience," I confess.

"Lester is here because of his ghost sight," LeClerc explains.

"How long have you guys been here?" I ask.

"I've been here a week, LeClerc three days and Lester came this morning," Brad informs me.

"So you haven't started training yet?"

"Not formal training. I have been working out and watched some of the videos in our room. There is some crazy shit on those videos," LeClerc informs.

Our order is up so we have dinner. We chat about insignificant things getting to know each other a little. After dinner, we return to our rooms. My luggage is in my room so I unpack and go to sleep early.

Chapter Ten:
Visions

During the night, I have a nightmare about Lilly and Tina being in my apartment in Kansas City. I see them going around my apartment looking at and touching my things. I see Lilly pick up a picture of Brian and me and hand it to Tina. I see Lilly and Tina go to my bed and smell it. They go to my closet and smell my clothes. Tina takes out a shirt that is Brian's and smells it then hands it to Lilly who also smells it. Lilly hands Brian's shirt back to Tina nodding yes to her. The vision is so real I can smell Brian's scent as well. They leave my apartment with the picture and Brian's shirt. As the door closes, I'm trapped in my apartment. I can hear Brian calling to me from outside but I can't open the door. Blood starts to pour into the apartment from around the door. I go to the windows to try and open them but more blood comes in around them. Soon I am drowning in blood. I awake screaming and soaked in sweat.

As I try to stop myself from shaking my door flies open and two men with automatic weapons and laser sights sweep my room.

"Are you all right, ma'am?" One of the men asks.

"I...will be. It ...was a nightmare. Can I speak to...Agent Smith?" I ask.

"I am sure he is asleep. Is it important enough to wake him?" the armed man questions.

I think for a moment. Lilly and Tina are going after Brian. Did that really happen as I saw it or was it just a nightmare. I'm not sure but I have to be sure. It could mean Brian's life or death. I have to have my apartment checked.

"Yes. I need to talk to him now," I demand still shaking a little.

One of the men leaves while the other watches over me. He is ready for anything and I see the safety is flipped off on his weapon. The other man comes back in a few minutes.

"Agent Smith is on his way. We are to wait with you until he comes. Is there anything we can get you?" the armed man asks.

"Can you turn around for a minute so I can put some pants on please?" I hope, since I'm still in bed just wearing a t-shirt and panties.

"Yes, ma'am," they say and turn around.

I pull on some pants and change my sweat soaked shirt. I curl up in my comfy chair with a blanket and wait. The guards relax but stay alert.

Agent Smith shows up around forty minutes later and dismisses the guards. He comes in my room holding a coffee cup and shuts the door. He gets my desk chair and sits down across from me. I can smell his steaming hot coffee and wished I had asked for some from the guards now. He waits for me to start talking.

"I had a nightmare that Lilly and Tina were in my apartment. They searched the place and took two items. A picture of Brian and me and a shirt of Brian's that had not been washed and has his scent on it. I know it was probably just a nightmare but I need for you to see if my apartment was broken into and if those two items are missing," I say looking at Agent Smith hoping he will follow up on it.

"Write down what the items looked like and exactly where they were in the apartment. Do it now. I'll be right back," Agent Smith orders.

I do as I'm asked. Agent Smith comes back in to the room and looks over what I have written on the paper. He nods to me and leaves the room again. I sit there waiting for about ten minutes. I wonder if Agent Smith is even coming back. Just as I'm about to go look for him, Agent Smith shows back up with a phone in his hand.

"Tell him to calm down," Agent Smith says, handing me the phone.

"Hello?"

"Becket? Is that you? Thank God. What the hell is going on?" Brian pleads.

"Just calm down and do what they tell you. The one I told you about is in town and knows about you. Calm down, honey. It'll be ok," I reassure, trying not to cry myself.

"I woke up and these men were in my room. They had guns and made me get dressed and go with them. They said they were with the FBI and worked with you. Now I'm in the backseat of a car with these men. Where are they taking me?" Brian mutters, obviously freaked out.

"They will keep you safe. You do exactly what they tell you to do. I know this is difficult but please do this for me. I'll call you when I can. Do what you are told, stay calm and you will be safe. I love you," I vow, welling up with emotion.

"I love you too, Becket, but this is all messed up. Call me soon," Brian begs and the line goes dead.

"Thank you for believing me," is all I can mumble to Agent Smith as I start to cry. I know it is unprofessional but this is just too much.

"Your apartment was broken into tonight. The items you described are missing. Tina's fingerprints were found as well as what we believe to be Lilly's fingerprints. Please explain to me about how you knew what happened within your apartment," Agent Smith demands looking right at me.

I wipe away tears and try to get my emotions under control. I look at Agent Smith and wonder what I should tell him.

"My family has some history with knowing things no one could possibly know. I have never dreamed something so vivid before. I just knew it was real," I reveal, speaking truthfully.

"You are speaking of your mother's family, correct?" Agent Smith asks.

"Yes, the Degano family from Italy," I confirm.

"Have you ever had other visions or experiences before?" Agent Smith asks.

"Yes."

"You are going to have to elaborate on those powers, however, that can wait for another time. Here is my phone number on the facility. You may use it from the phone over at your desk. The phone does not dial off the base so do not try. Please call me if you have any more visions. Goodnight, Becket," Agent Smith smiles.

"Thank you, Agent Smith. Goodnight."

I think about what just occurred. Agent Smith was not surprised at all that I had a vision. He once told me I had a very interesting family on my mother's side. I wonder how much he knows about that side of my family. Almost anyone in Degano Valley would acknowledge Gran has the sight, and many whisper about her using the evil eye. He could have found out during his background check on me. Well, all that really matters is that Brian is safe. I crawl back in bed and try to get some sleep.

Chapter Eleven:
Good Boy or Bad Boy

The next morning at 6 a.m., my video screen comes on by itself and plays reveille waking me. God, I am tired. I was up most of the night after my nightmare. I just want to roll over and go back to sleep but I know that's not an option. I go to the end of my hall to the showers, then, I get dressed in the camo-fatigues and make my way to breakfast at about 6:30 a.m. Brad and Lester both look as tired as I feel. Only LeClerc seems to be chipper and ready to go. We have breakfast and walk to our training area at 7 a.m. Today we are meeting in a small room with several monitors along the walls. Hawkins is in the room waiting for us when we arrive.

"We will meet in this room every morning at 7 a.m. unless I give you other instructions. If you are late, you will be punished. Do you understand?" Hawkins demands.

"Yes, sir," LeClerc, Brad and I say. Lester just looks at Hawkins as if he is some alien being.

"Today is all about orientation. I will explain our facility and where you are allowed to go. You will be restricted to this floor for most of your training. We will do a few exercises on the surface and a couple on level two of this facility. You are not allowed to go anywhere else. You are not allowed to contact anyone outside this facility. If you are caught violating these rules you will be disciplined. Do you understand?" Hawkins asks.

"Yes, sir," LeClerc, Brad and I reply. Lester also says it this time and butchers a salute.

Hawkins goes over the procedure for getting through security, the layout of the areas we are allowed into and our daily schedule. He talks to us about the security in place around the facility and the security force known as Hounds as in HEL Hounds, the watchdogs of Hades. We learn how to fill out paperwork and do daily video logs.

Over the next two weeks everyone falls into step training, even Lester. It is clear that only LeClerc and I have any formal law enforcement training. LeClerc is on par with me in hand-to-hand combat but his style is all about force where mine is about speed and agility. LeClerc is a slightly better shot than I am, with Lester not being too far behind me. Brad is not at home with a gun but is able to pass the course. It appears to me that Brad will mainly be a researcher and not in the field that often.

One night at dinner, LeClerc tells me a little about his past.

"I was born in Switzerland. My mother was Swiss and my father French. I was raised as an altar boy, but I always got into trouble," LeClerc says, smiling at me.

"What kind of trouble?" I smile back at him.

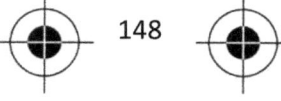

"Some of the boys would tease me about being an altar boy and how I had to turn the other cheek. I showed them I preferred the God full of vengeance as he was in the Old Testament, so I got into a lot of fights. I was good at it and even liked it. My parents were killed in a car crash when I was twelve and I became a ward of the church. Needless to say, my fighting and bad attitude just got worse," LeClerc confesses.

"I can't imagine losing my parents even now. We are pretty close," I reveal.

"There was a local Bishop who took me under his wing. He straightened me out enough to get me into the Swiss Guard. I flourished within the military and my bishop still favored me. When he moved to Italy as an Archbishop, he took me with him as a personal bodyguard. He later arranged for me to join the Pontifical Swiss Guard who guard the pope. After a few years serving the pope I was once again assigned to my Archbishop who had become unpopular with the Mafia for his protection of the common man," LeClerc explains.

"I just can't see you guarding the pope. You are making that part up, aren't you?" I tease LeClerc.

"What I tell you is all true. My Archbishop was attacked, I fought as well as I could, I killed several men but one would just not die. That one was a vampire. He killed my Archbishop and left me for dead. I hope to one day catch up to that vampire so I can kill him," LeClerc vows.

We finish our dinner and LeClerc walks me back to my room as he often does. I know he wants to come in but I never offer.

LeClerc keeps pushing my boundaries with a comment here and a slight touch there. He wants to be with me and the bad thing is, I want to be with him. This training is stressful and it would be nice to just roll around the bed for a while. But then I think of Brian and I know I can't.

About three weeks into our training, LeClerc walks me back from dinner and follows me into my room. When I turn to see what he wants, he kisses me deep and meaningfully. LeClerc's scent fills my head as his large hands pull my body into his. I return LeClerc's desperate kiss. I want him!

LeClerc grabs my shirt and starts to rip it off. Somehow, this wakes me from my animal desires and I forcefully push him away from me hard. The tearing of my shirt still in LeClerc's hand followed by the loud crash of LeClerc's body against my closed door awakens me even further. I look at him standing in front of me like a hungry animal. Oh, how I want to forget Brian and just have LeClerc. Being with Brian was always safe, tender and loving, even in the beginning of our relationship. LeClerc is all but tender and safe.

"You have to go," I stammer, finally finding my voice.

"Are you sure?"

"No, but you have to go," I concede, not sure myself.

"Another time," LeClerc vows, smiling at me. He blows me a kiss and leaves. I go to my door and lock it.

Over the next week, the sexual tension between LeClerc and me intensifies. He touches me several times a day and his looks drive me insane. His stolen touches are small like rubbing his hand along my arm as he walks by me or coming up behind me and placing his hand on my shoulder or waist. Each touch seems innocent enough but they drive me crazy. My resolve to stay true to Brian is being tested several times a day. I'm afraid that LeClerc is succeeding in wearing me down. If he came into my room again, I don't think I would have the strength to make him leave. I dream about him coming into my room at night. I'm distracted in my classes, and my training is suffering. I need to do something.

After dinner, I decide what I need to do. I'm not sure it is the right thing but I want to try. I call Agent Smith.

"Hi, I'm sorry to bother you but I need a favor," I say, still wondering if I'm doing the right thing.

"What do you want, Becket?" Agent Smith asks.

"I need to talk to Brian," I hesitate.

"I told you Brian is safe. Have you had another vision?" Agent Smith questions.

"No, but I need to speak to Brian. It is a personal matter," I reveal.

"Meet me at the elevator in ten minutes," Agent Smith sighs.

I pace my room for eight minutes then head to the elevator. My keycard will not even work the elevator. I am trapped on this floor. I never felt trapped in HEL until now. I wonder why I'm freaking out. I just need to talk to Brian and then everything will be ok. It has to be. I cannot lose Brian. He's the best thing that has ever happened to me. Nevertheless, I'm only twenty-two years old, how many things have even happened to me. How do I know, LeClerc might be great for me? I know he would be great for an hour or two. After that, I have no idea. How do we ever know? Just then, the elevator doors open and Agent Smith is standing there.

"Come with me, Becket," Agent Smith orders.

"I'm not allowed off this floor," I inform Agent Smith.

"I understand that. However, you are allowed to go places with me. Get in the damn elevator," Agent Smith demands seeming to be annoyed and tired.

We go up to the garage and walk to one of the smaller building about half a mile from the garage. I see a couple of the Hounds on patrol. They acknowledge our presence with a nod of the head. We go inside. I know exactly where we are.

"Welcome to my home, Becket. Make yourself comfortable over there in the living room," Agent Smith smiles.

The house appears comfortable and easy to live in. The kitchen/dining room area flows into the living room, only separated by a nice bar. A hallway leads to a bathroom and two bedrooms or maybe a bedroom and an office. I sit in a recliner and watch Agent Smith go to the bar and make us both a gin and tonic. He brings one to me, sits down in another recliner, and sips on his drink.

"Tell me about what is going on with you," Agent Smith asks, sipping his drink.

"I need to know if Brian is ok and still loves me," I hesitate, feeling that is what I need.

"Why?"

"I need to be grounded again. I hope talking to Brian will do it," I admit, half hoping it will work and half-hoping he wants to call off the engagement.

"Are you questioning his commitment to you or your commitment to him?" Agent Smith probes, taking a sip of his drink.

I take a big sip of my drink and am startled by the strong taste. I use the drink to consider my answer before I speak.

"Both, but mostly my commitment to him," I reveal, realizing that I'm the one wanting to cheat on Brian.

"You fought to be able to keep Brian in your life. You told me you would be a better Agent if Brian was in your life, waiting for you, loving you. Now you are wavering on your commitment to him?" Agent Smith demands, looking directly at me, making me feel dirty.

"It's complicated. LeClerc is very attracted to me and I to him. I love Brian but I'm tempted by LeClerc," I confess, feeling bad just saying the words.

"Have you had sex with LeClerc?" Agent Smith inquires, very bluntly.

"No. We kissed once but I stopped it from going any further," I vow, feeling a throbbing pain in the pit of my stomach.

"So you figure you can hear Brian's voice and listen to him tell you he loves you and this thing with LeClerc will all just go away?" Agent Smith asks, with his best "are you crazy?" look.

"Well yeah. I hoped so. I guess I just don't know what to do," I admit, putting my hands over my face.

"Sounds like you want permission to be with LeClerc. You hope Brian will let you off the hook or you will feel comfortable that Brian is safe and better off without you so it would be OK if you cheated on him. What do you think?" Agent Smith accuses, as he gets up to refill his drink.

Damn, Agent Smith is probably right. No matter what Brian says, I most likely will still sleep with LeClerc. I am not a cheater. I have never slept with another person when I was in a relationship before. Why am I so attracted to LeClerc? What the hell am I going to do? Agent Smith probably thinks I'm just some damn PMSing wacko girl.

"So you going to dump Brian and marry LeClerc now?" Agent Smith pokes.

"NO!" I announce, a little too loud.

"So you are just going to be with LeClerc and never tell Brian. Is that it?"

"No," I hesitate, not even sure myself anymore.

"Third choice is you have sex with LeClerc but then tell Brian because you want to be forgiven for your betrayal. Brian has forgiven all the lies you've already told him what is a little cheating to a love like that. Is that your plan?" Agent Smith accuses, pushing me over the edge.

"NO! I hate that I want to be with LeClerc. I hate it," I snap, feeling disgusted with myself.

"You can choose to be with LeClerc or not. You can choose to be true to Brian or not. I understand that you are confused but you are the one in control of this situation, not LeClerc, and certainly not Brian," Agent Smith explains.

"LeClerc will never be more than a momentary distraction for you and you know it. That is why you have put him off this long. You know Brian would be better for you but he is only a memory and not constantly around you. I will not tell you what to do. This decision needs to be totally yours," Agent Smith forces.

I sip my drink a little and think about my situation. I know there would never be a future with LeClerc. I'm not sure I can ever truly have a future with anyone. Maybe that is what I'm afraid of. If I blow this chance with Brian, I will lose my connection to the Norm world. I'll become all about the job and can be with as many LeClercs as I want. It would be easier to not have to worry about Brian and the hope he brings to my life. It would not be better, but much easier. I have never been one to choose the easy way out before. Why should I start now?

"Can I talk to Brian?" I decide.

"That can be arranged, but I would like to talk some more first," Agent Smith tells me, looking down at his glass.

"OK."

"Would you like another drink?"

"Umm…ok," I agree, thinking something is up.

"I want you to tell me about your abilities with visions and such," Agent Smith probes, while he pours my drink.

There it is. He wants me to tell him about my gifts in exchange for talking to Brian. Just when I feel like we are starting to become friends, Agent Smith throws me off balance.

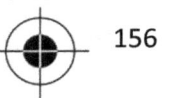

"Could I talk to Brian first?" I question, seeing if I am right.

"You could but I don't think you would want to talk to me about your abilities anymore. Am I correct?" Agent Smith asks.

"If you let me talk to Brian, I will tell you about my abilities," I agree, seeing if Agent Smith will trust me.

"OK. I was hoping we could do this tonight but I see it's not going to happen. Let's go," Agent Smith orders, as he puts down his drink and heads for the door.

I figure I messed up somehow but am not sure where. I follow Agent Smith out of the house and back towards the garage. After about a hundred feet, Agent Smith turns and heads to another house. Perhaps we will make the call from here. We walk up on the porch and stop.

"I expect you to keep your promise soon. I will see you at the elevator by 6:30 a.m. Not later, understand?" Agent Smith smiles, starting to walk away.

"What's going on? Is the phone inside the house?" I ask.

"No, Brian is inside the house," Agent Smith reveals.

I turn and look at the door. Brian is behind this door. He is right here. All I have to do is open the door and I'll be with Brian. I wonder how long he has been here. I reach for the door handle and everything seems to move in slow motion. I turn the handle and hear music playing. I slowly walk inside and Brian is standing by the bar with two glasses of red wine beside him. He slowly moves towards me as I more towards him. I have to get to him. I have to have his arms around me. I will die without his love to reenergize me. We are moving so slow. I'm frantic in my need to touch Brian. To be with him. I feel the very air pushing against me and I force my body to move towards Brian. Brian is moving to me as slowly as I am to him. I know this stillness is illusion but at this moment, it is my reality.

After what seems like forever, we finally touch and the slow motion movement vanishes into hasty desperate need. After what seems like hours, we drift off to sleep in each other's arms. We have hardly spoken but have said so much to each other just being together.

The damn video monitor flips on at 6 a.m. screaming its unwanted wake up call. Brian and I both long to remain in bed. I kiss Brian and make my way to the shower. I shampoo my hair and I'm overcome by the strawberry fragrance that reminds me so much of being at home in Brian's little house. He uses this same kind of shampoo. I remember teasing him about it being girly. I know the strawberry smell will linger with me all day and remind me of Brian.

I hear the video play another round of unwanted interruption and I know it is 6:15 a.m. and I have to meet Agent Smith in 15 minutes. I quickly towel off and get dressed. I kiss Brian franticly as if I'll never see him again. He holds me and I feed on his love. I'm amazed how much I need to be with him. It just feels so right.

"I fall you, Brian. I love you. But I have to go," I say, basking in Brian's loving gaze.

"I love you. I fall you, my lovely Becket. Go and do your job. I'll be here waiting," Brian vows.

"I don't know when I will be back. I need you and love you so much," I confess, not wanting to leave Brian.

"I know you will see me when you can. I love you," Brian whispers, kissing me goodbye.

Just then, the next alarm screams that it is 6:30 a.m. and I know I'm late.

"I have to go. I'm already late. I love you, Brian," I wave, as I leave the little house.

The morning is foggy and I don't like the cool wet feel of the outside world. I was so warm and comfortable inside with Brian. I run towards the garage but dare a glance backwards and see Brian standing on the porch waving at me and blowing me kisses. I blow a kiss to him and keep running. I turn into the garage and see Agent Smith standing inside the elevator waiting. I run in the elevator and hug Agent Smith, who seems to not know what to do.

"Thank you so much for letting me see Brian. I really needed that," I thank, as I let go my hug.

"You are very welcome Becket," Agent Smith says, seeming a little surprised at my perkiness.

"You wanted to know about my abilities. Well I can touch..." I start to reveal but Agent Smith interrupts me.

"We will talk about that later. You need to grab some breakfast before your training starts. Do not mention what happened up top," Agent Smith orders.

I nod and lose a bit of my enthusiasm. I wonder why Agent Smith does not want me to tell him about my powers right now. I cannot believe it is that he wants me to get a good breakfast. I glance up at the camera watching us in the elevator. Is that the reason? Maybe Agent Smith does not want the description of my abilities taped. Then that would mean he was not planning to share them with all the rest of the staff here at HEL. Why would he do that?

The elevator doors open and Agent Smith lets me out. I see him push the fifth button. What is on that floor? I really don't know that much about this facility or Agent Smith. I do know that Agent Smith brought Brian here to be with me, so that earns him a lot of leeway in my book.

Throughout the day, LeClerc makes suggestive comments and touches me but has little effect. Brian's shield of love is renewed around me and blocks all LeClerc's attempts to seduce me. A few times during the day, I catch a whiff of strawberry and I smile thinking of Brian. I cannot believe Brian is here. I did not even ask him how he got here or how long he has been here. I'm such a bad person.

Chapter Twelve: Abilities

After dinner, I walk back to my room and find Agent Smith waiting for me. He motions me to follow him and we go to the elevator. We travel up, through the garage and to his house. I watch Brian's house every second hoping to get a glimpse of him through a window as we walk by. I am disappointed when I see no sign of him. We go into Agent Smith's home and make ourselves comfortable.

"Now you can tell me about your abilities, Becket," Agent Smith says.

"Are you trying to hide my abilities from someone inside HEL?" I ask.

"Let's just say I want to know what they are before we disclose them," Agent Smith admits.

"Is there some reason I should be concerned for myself or Brian from HEL?" I ask, wondering what Agent Smith is worried about.

"Not currently, but that could change if your special gifts were known. I will know better when I know exactly what your abilities are," Agent Smith confesses.

"I can deal with supernatural threats or threats from Norms, but I don't want to have to worry about the people I work with becoming a threat. That is not what I signed up for," I accuse, really starting to worry.

"I understand and feel the same as you do. For a reason that still eludes me, I have endangered myself by taking a personal interest in you. It is known within HEL that I am watching out for you. This makes us both more high profile, but gives me the opportunity to help you, such as bringing Brian here. That was not a popular decision. My motives are being questioned," Agent Smith admits.

"Have you endangered your life, or just your position in the organization?" I question, wondering how serious this is.

"For now, it is all political. I will benefit from you doing well and take a hit if you fail. There is much discussion over my motives. There are rumors that we are lovers. You spending time with Brian will alleviate some of those rumors but then they will have to come up with another reason. I want you to know that I have done nothing to squelch the rumors of us being lovers. It is something that can be explained and though frowned upon, it is acceptable," Agent Smith confesses.

"I want to completely understand your gifts so I can recommend a course of action to you, and decide whether to reveal them or not. You are currently believed to be an outstanding up and coming agent. One who will be an asset to HEL. We need to make sure the perception stays that way," Agent Smith explains.

"You choose to talk about it here because we are not being monitored. Is that correct?" I ask.

"Yes. You should assume you are always under surveillance, even when you are with Brian. I have swept Brian's house several times and each time I find new devices. Brian is an outsider and not trusted," Agent Smith admits.

"What can I tell Brian?" I ask.

"Your original story. A mass murderer is hunting you. Do not disclose the layout or location of the underground facility, or even that it is underground. Do not go into any of the training in detail. He is here to keep him safe and give you the support you need. From your interaction with LeClerc, I was wondering if I even did the right thing by bringing Brian here," Agent Smith reveals.

"You knew I was attracted to LeClerc before I came to you about it?"

"Yes. I told you to assume you are always being monitored," Agent Smith reminds.

"So you spied on me?" I accuse, feeling completely violated.

"Yes. I am one of a few people who go over video footage of new trainees," Agent Smith admits.

"You must have seen me struggling with LeClerc. Why did you not come and tell me Brian was here?" I demand, starting to get a little mad.

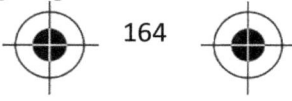

"I told you that you are the only one who could make the decision to be with LeClerc or Brian. It is not my place to dictate your personal life. Brian arrived six days ago. I knew you were close to making your decision between Brian and LeClerc. I wanted Brian here in case you needed him. I did what I could to help you, without directly interfering. I let you make the decision," Agent Smith explains, getting up to make a drink.

"I'm sorry. You have done more for me than I know. I thank you for that. But, I don't like the idea of being spied on," I admit, wondering why Agent Smith has put his career in jeopardy to help me.

"You are in training and being monitored. You should expect that. You know you were monitored at the Farm and even at Quantico. Spying, as you call it, is just part of the process to see how the recruit is handling pressure, how they interact with their other students and teachers," Agent Smith clarifies, taking a sip of his drink and nodding to himself at its taste.

"I know all that, but I do not think I should be watched in my bedroom, or expect every action to be analyzed. I have just never had it put right in my face before," I admit, kind of feeling uncomfortable about the subject.

"Let us move on to your gifts, shall we?" Agent Smith redirects, taking a seat across from me.

"Ok. I can touch an object and get visions of important moments in its existence. The more emotion around the object at a specific instance, the stronger the vision of that time. When I first touched Lilly's doll, I saw a vision of her mother around 1900 giving it to Lilly. A vampire decapitated Lilly's mother before attacking Lilly. I knew that doll was very important to Lilly from my vision so I threatened to hurt the doll to hold Lilly at bay until the sun came up and I could get away," I tell an amazed Agent Smith.

"That is a wonderful gift. It runs in your family, correct?" Agent Smith asks.

"Yes, my Gran and her mother had that gift. I see you have researched my family," I say, confirming my suspicions and wondering what else he knows.

"Your family is known to me. Our European office has a file on the Degano family that even mentions you," Agent Smith reveals.

"What does it say?"

"It states that you should be watched to see if you possess the sight. However, it talks about several of the women in your family having the sight and something called the evil eye. The most interesting part about your family is Antal Degano. Have you ever met him?" Agent Smith probes.

"Yes. When I was sixteen he came to my Gran's house to talk with me," I say, remembering the night long ago.

"What was your impression of him?" Agent Smith inquires.

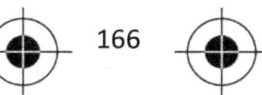

"He was too young to have as much power and respect as he did. He was mysterious and knew much about me. He wanted me to make Degano Valley my home and I think work with him. He had a silver cane that I touched and lost myself in a vision of blood. I was in a coma for a month working my way out of the vision of drowning blood I experienced when I touched Antal's cane. I lost my gift to see visions from objects then but it returned when I touched Lilly's doll," I explain, remembering those horrible events.

"Do you know anything else about Antal?" Agent Smith asks.

"After I met Lilly I started to have nightmares about Lilly and Tina. They always ended with me drowning in blood. This made me think about Antal. I believe now that Antal is a vampire."

"The file on your family is not as detailed as your intimate knowledge but it does suggest the possibility of Antal Degano being a vampire. The first record of an Antal Degano dates back to 1612. That Antal is probably an ancestor of the current one but the name pops up several times over the years. The possibility that the original Antal may be the one you met at your grandmother's house has to be considered. I have not shared what I found about your family with HEL. I think we should leave it that way unless you want to go hunting Antal," Agent Smith says seriously.

"No, I have no wish to hunt members of my family," I admit.

"Do you have any other gifts?" Agent Smith inquires.

"I can sense when I am in danger. Kind of like Spiderman's danger sense," I joke.

"You really possess a danger sense?"

"Yes. I know when I am in threat of physical harm, and somewhat the degree of the threat. In a fight I can anticipate my opponent's actions before they happen," I confide.

"No wonder you are top of the class in all the hand-to-hand combat training. That is a great ability to have," Agent Smith replies enviously. "Do you possess any other gifts?"

"Well you were there the first time I had a dream vision about Lilly and Tina going through my apartment. I'm not sure if that is a new gift or a onetime thing," I confess.

"Ok, I don't think we should mention these gifts to anyone. They will prove very useful to you in the field so use them, but do not reveal them even to your partners. Do you understand?" Agent Smith cautions me very seriously.

"Yes, I understand. I have hidden them all my life. You are the first person I have told outside my mother's family," I confide.

"Good. That is all I wanted to talk to you about. Is there anything else you wish to chat about?"

"What is going to happen to Brian?"

"Well that is partly up to you. Do you want him around? You still thinking of marrying Brian?" Agent Smith inquires.

"Yes, I definitely want him around."

"He can't live here unless he is officially brought into HEL. You have indicated you do not want to do that. Am I correct?"

"No, I don't want him to be involved in all this."

"Then I believe the best thing would be for him to get a job in a closer town. His house in Kansas City is known to Lilly so he should not go back there. I could arrange a job for him within about an hour drive of here, in Rolla, MO." Agent Smith explains.

"That sounds like a great plan. Then I would be near HEL when not working cases and could go home weekends," I agree, thinking this will work out great.

"You cannot tell Brian where this facility is located. He thinks this is just a safe house and not a full facility. Let's keep it that way. You can spend tonight with Brian. Then he is gone. I will arrange for his new job and a house for you two in Rolla. This is a big investment in you, so don't let me down," Agent Smith says half smiling at me, but I know he is also serious.

"Can I tell Brian about the Rolla job and house thing?"

"Yes, but don't talk about how close it is to here. He will be led to believe he is now much further away from Rolla than he really is,"

"Ok, will do," I smile getting up.

"Yes, you can go see Brian now," Agent Smith chuckles to himself at my eagerness.

"Thank you again." I leave Agent Smith's house.

I hurry over to the guest house. Brian quickly answers the door and I go inside. We kiss and kiss. I know I wanted to talk to Brian but the moment takes me and an hour passes.

"I fall you," I whisper into Brian's ear.

"I fall you, Becket," Brian breathes back to me.

Brian is drifting and in danger of falling to sleep. I climb off him and get him to sit up on the couch.

"We need to talk a little before we go to bed. This will be our last night together for a while," I confess, sitting next to Brian.

"Where am I going this time?"

"Kansas City is too dangerous for us to live in at the moment. We are going to get a house in Rolla. A new job is being arranged for you as well. I will call you when I can and come to you soon."

"I must really love you to move to Rolla," Brian jokes, but he's worried.

From what little I know of Rolla it is about two hours to the closest large city. It is in the middle of nowhere on a major highway. Rolla has a population of less than twenty thousand. It is home to the Missouri University of Science and Technology, which is the main draw of the town. Even though it has the university, Rolla has a small town country feel to it.

"I know it is away from your house, friends and family but it will be closer to where I work so that will be good," I apologize, searching Brian's eyes for what he is really feeling.

"I am sure it will work out. Can't be worse than the last few weeks. I've been taken to four different safe houses in that time. I sure am thankful we had this time together. Just promise me this will all be over soon. I'm not like you. I need some consistency to my life," Brian complains.

"I have to be with you. I was feeling so lost. I need my Brian time. I will do everything I can to get us back to a more normal life," I smile at Brian.

Brian starts kissing me and then leads me to bed. Well I guess that was enough talking anyway.

Chapter Thirteen:
The Trap

During the rest of my training, I am scheduled to spend every other weekend with Brian in Rolla. This is my recharge time and I cherish it. Brian gets a job working for a Government Geological group doing computer work. He likes the work and the pay and benefits are even better than his old job. The house we move into is a nice ranch style with a lot of room. I notice that it has a very sophisticated alarm system. The intruder alert security makes me worry that maybe even here we are not safe.

Agent Smith has arranged for Brian to live under a false last name while in Rolla. He was concerned that Tina might be smart enough to track him down by his real name. Brian is not pleased about the idea, but goes along.

One night about two months into my training, I have another vision. I see Lilly and Tina standing outside the storage locker where I parked my car. Little six-year-old Lilly grabs the garage door and opens it shearing the heavy-duty lock clean off. I see the two of them going through my car. They smell the seats and what little stuff is left in the car. They then turn and walk to the place I went through the fence. They go through the fence and stop where Agent Smith picked me up in his car. They smell the air and even the road. Lilly examines the few rocks on the road and picks up a few of them. They both look down the road the way Agent Smith drove off. It is as if they are looking at me. I fall into the road, which has turned to blood. I am thrashing in the blood trying to keep my head above it. I am drowning in blood. I awake screaming in my room at the HEL underground facility.

Guards burst into my room a few moments later and sweep the room. I tell them it was a nightmare. They leave after making sure the room is clear. I then pick up the phone and call Agent Smith.

"What is so important at 3 a.m.?" Agent Smith's sleepily mumbles.

"I had another nightmare," I say, not wanting to say too much since I know I am being monitored.

"And you want to talk, super. I will meet you in the elevator in fifteen," Agent Smith sighs and the line goes dead.

Agent Smith and I go back to his house to talk.

"Lilly and Tina have found the car I dropped off in storage at Carthage, MO. They appeared to be tracking your car next," I hurriedly state.

"Ok, I have to think about this one," Agent Smith yawns.

"Let's set a trap for them at the house we stayed in after Carthage. It's secluded and they have tracked me everywhere else. It should be a total surprise," I exclaim, thinking it is about time for a little bit of payback.

"That could work. Let me study and plan it up and get back to you about it. I am not sure you will be allowed to participate, but I will try to get you involved."

"I want to be there for the trap. I am the one she is after," I admit, hoping I will be included.

"I understand but we don't know when they will appear only where. They took almost two months to go from Kansas City to Carthage. Who knows how long it will take them. I will formulate a plan and pass it by the higher ups. Let's get you back to bed," Agent Smith smiles.

I know Agent Smith has a point about timing but this is our best opportunity to capture or kill Lilly and Tina. Agent Smith escorts me back to the elevator and I go back to bed.

Two days later a mission briefing in the conference room interrupts our training. Agent Smith is the one in charge. The senior staff attends through video conference along the wall. The seats of the conference table are filled with LeClerc, ten of the Hounds security personnel, Chad Easley head of security for this HEL facility, Agent Smith and myself.

"We have an opportunity to capture two vampires. One is named Tina Wilson. Her photos are displayed on the monitors. She has been a vampire for around two years. She is to be considered extremely dangerous. If she cannot be contained, deadly force is authorized," Agent Smith explains.

"The other vampire is Lilly. See the sketches of her on the monitor. She may look like a six-year-old little girl but she is known to have killed several people extremely violently. She is believed to be over one hundred years old. Do not underestimate her. Deadly force is authorized if she cannot be contained."

"It should be noted that Lilly always travels with a doll. This doll is very important to her and can be used against her. If shooting Lilly fails as a deterrent, shoot the doll and Lilly should react. Only do this if you want to draw her full wrath. Threatening to hurt the doll or using it as a hostage is the best course of action. I know it sounds crazy but a hundred year old psycho six-year-old vampire is pretty crazy also."

"There is a slight possibility that the two vampires will be accompanied by one Corky. See the monitor for his image. We are not sure if he is a servant of Lilly or a vampire. He is a known associate so should be assumed to travel with them. If he is a servant he will be able to travel during daylight so be prepared for that," Agent Smith continues.

"We know a location where these two vampires are going. We, however, do not know when it will occur. It will most likely be in the next couple of weeks. We will rotate shifts to stay at the house. A team will stay four days on location at a time, then switch. Each team will be made up of five Hounds, one new Agent and one special Agent. Easley will lead the team with LeClerc and I will lead the team with Becket. My team will be known as Alpha team, Easley's team will be called Bravo."

"During the day you will sleep and work on putting in ultraviolet lights and securing the area. The vampires will obviously only come at night but remember they may have a Norm servant," Agent Smith notes.

"Becket has encountered these vampires on two different occasions and survived. She is to be consulted on tactics if time permits. Her firsthand information should be very valuable in the field."

"Alpha team will leave the compound at 7 a.m. tomorrow. This afternoon get your gear ready for the operation. All the specifics about the OP are in the files in front of you. Any Questions?" Agent Smith pauses.

No one immediately asks a question so Agent Smith dismisses us to get ready. The rest of the day, I help pack three large bulletproof SUV's full of gear. We are going in way heavy on gear and firepower. From my training, I learned that HEL has never captured a live vampire and only confirmed the destruction of five of them. Therefore, this opportunity is huge for the HEL staff. They do not want to mess it up.

We are all issued Blasters, which are small handheld flamethrowers. They are good at a range of

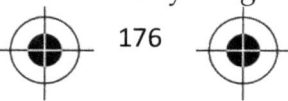

up to two meters. Fire is the only sure way of killing a vampire that is known beside sunlight. One of the Hounds is also issued a full size flamethrower. We are all issued weapons with High Explosive Incendiary/Armor Piercing Ammunition (HEIAP). Impact ignites the incendiary material in the tip, triggering the high explosive charge. The second incendiary charge is also ignited. The incendiary charge burns at over 1000 degrees Celsius, is hard to extinguish, and lasts almost ten minutes. Should do quite a lot of damage, even to vampires. It is my understanding that HEIAP ammo and flamethrowers are outlawed from use by the international phosphorus weapons ban, which has been signed by many nations including the U.S. Whether these weapons are banned or not, I am glad we are going to have them when Lilly and Tina come around.

The only theorized way to immobilize a vampire is to drive a shaft of wood into its heart. We have all had extensive archery practice with bow and crossbow. We have also done numerous drills of fighting hand-to-hand with stakes and then thrusting them home into specially designed dummies. We take bows, crossbows and stakes along to try first. The heavy firepower is in case immobilization of the vampires fail.

The next morning we make the hour drive to the safe house where Lilly and Tina should be tracking me to. We spend the day preparing the house for an attack. All the doors and windows are set with motion sensors. Outside cameras and motion sensors are placed all around the house and even on surrounding trees. We get the main living room wired with ultraviolent lights before night falls.

The wind picks up and the swaying of the tall grass and tree branches keeps setting off the motion detectors. We have several false alarms but no sign of Lilly and Tina. The next day we recalibrate the motion detectors to pick up movement but not go off at the slightest sway of a branch.

The next three nights a sensor goes off here or there but no sign of intruders. We return to base when Bravo team under Easley takes over. I go back to training and find it hard to sleep at night wondering what is going on out at the safe house. In the conference room, I am able to watch and listen to Bravo team. All the cameras, motion detectors and mics of the men register in this room twenty-four hours a day. Everything is recorded and stored for later evaluation.

I miss my weekend with Brian as my rotation with the Alpha team goes over our weekend. I hate to admit it but the waiting really gets to you after a while and we get a little lax. Agent Smith does what he can to keep us on our toes. Since I have a personal interest in this matter, I more than anyone, should be on my guard but it is hard just waiting for anything at all to happen.

By my fourth rotation, it has been over a month and still no sign of Lilly or Tina. Everyone, including Agent Smith, is frustrated. We have now gone on a rotation of three people on watch until 1 a.m., then the other four on watch until sunrise. It is not the best way, but it keeps the men a bit more sane. From what I understand, Easley's team still stand watch together every night. He is a hard taskmaster who prides himself on always being prepared.

The last night of our fourth rotation, I am to stand second watch and be awoken at 1 a.m. I have a nightmare of Lilly and Tina watching the house. They walk around the house and see the SUVs parked in the garage. I can see Lilly move in the blink of an eye from the garage to the front door. I see Lilly whispering and motioning to one of the Hounds inside. I watch as the Hound goes to the door, deactivates the alarm and opens the door. Lilly pounces on him when he opens the door and blood pours out of him. I begin to choke and know I am drowning in blood. I awake sitting straight up in bed covered in sweat.

I immediately pick up my headset and speak into it.

"Lilly and Tina are in the house. At least one Hound has been killed by the front door. This is not a drill, I repeat, vampires are in the house," I inform, as I grab my gun and Blaster.

"All units converge on the front door," Agent Smith orders.

I go into the hallway and head for the stairs down to the main floor.

A hound reports, "Coming to the front door. Holy shit...there is blood everywhere. Where is his head? Oh my God, they took his head. Holy...," screams fill the mic, then nothing but silence.

"Stay calm people and get to the living room," Agent Smith commands.

A Hound coming into the hall in front of me startles me. I almost shoot at the movement and could have killed him. He sees me and we go down the stairs together.

"I'm in the living room. It's all clear," one of the Hounds reports over the mic.

The Hound I'm with is leading the way. We get to the bottom of the stairs and he lets go with his gun at something I cannot see.

"POP, POP, POP..." the Hounds gun reports as he goes full auto.

"Ahhh..." I hear a woman scream and it sounds familiar. It is Tina screaming. The Hound must be shooting her.

"POP, POP, POP..." the Hounds gun keeps going.

I try to move into a better position on the steps but just do not have a good shot. I see the Hound raising his gun in the air. Tina has leaped into the air and lands on top of the Hound. She grabs him by the base

of his neck and twists it clean off him in one fluid motion. She hungrily laps up the blood pouring from the Hound's severed head as I start to unload my clip into her.

"BANG, BANG, BANG…" my pistol goes, sending HEIAP rounds into Tina.

The hair on the back of my neck is standing straight up and I know I am in extreme danger.

"Need backup at the bottom of the stairs," I shout as I keep shooting Tina.

Tina turns on me. I have to do something, as my bullets are not stopping her fast enough. I can see the burning wounds in her body. I see three of the burning bullets expel themselves from her body as I'm shooting her full of new bullets. Her ability to heal is incredible.

I drop my gun and pull out my Blaster as Tina scrambles up the stairs to me. I unleash the torrent of fire right onto Tina.

"Ahhh…ahhh…ahhh," Tina screams like nothing I have ever heard before.

She is in extreme agony. I can see her skin bubbling and bursting under the spout of fire. My nostrils are filled with the horrid smell of burning flesh and hair. Tina scrambles over me knocking me to the floor. My Blaster flame hits the wall setting it on fire. I switch it off and look after Tina who disappears up the stairs.

The wall is on fire but it isn't a large area. If I can put it out soon the house can be saved. I take out my knife, cut a large piece of carpet out of the stairs, and use it to smother the flames.

"Ahhh…ahhh…ahhh," I hear coming from Tina as the upstairs shower turns on.

Tina must be putting herself out and trying to sooth her burns. I need to get after her but we will lose the house if this fire is not put out. A Hound appears at the bottom of the stairs and comes up to help me with the fire. I still hear Tina's screams coming from the upstairs shower.

"The guns barely slow them down. Use the Blasters at close range," I explain into my mic.

The Hound and I get the fire under control and head upstairs to find Tina.

"A Hound and I are heading up stairs to get Tina. She is very hurt from a point blank Blaster attack. We think she is in the upstairs bathroom," I inform to the Hound next to me and anyone still alive to listen to my mic.

The Hound goes first up the stairs. We both have our Blasters out. We creep down the hallway to the closed bathroom door. The Hound signals me that he is going to open the door and step to the side so I can spray Tina with fire. I nod my understanding of the plan but am worried since I do not hear any sound coming from the bathroom but the shower.

The Hound flings the bathroom door open and I let out a swath of flame from my blaster right into the shower. The shower curtain burst into flames and

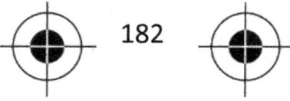

melts onto the floor. I see Tina is not in the shower and switch off my blaster as I hear something behind me.

I turn and a charred Tina has the Hound I was with in her grasp and is drinking greedily from him. I freeze for a moment as I watch some of Tina's wounds heal right before my eyes.

"Becket report on your situation," Agent Smith's demanding voice comes into my ear.

The voice in my ear snaps me out of my trance and I unleash a torrent of flame onto Tina and the Hound in her arms.

"Ahhh…ahhh…ahhh," the Hound and Tina scream.

It is a truly horrible sight to watch someone burn to death. A moment ago, this man was my comrade in arms, now his skin is boiling and cracking from the fire I directed at him. All his hair burns off and assaults me with its putrid smell. My eyes water from the heat and intense odor wafting from the burning bodies. I know Tina's bite probably would have killed him but my bathing him in flame surely will.

Tina is writhing in agony and falls to the floor as my Blaster runs out of fuel. I pull out a stake and drive it through her chest into her heart. It is damn hard to get that piece of wood into a body. I have to put all my weight on it and wiggle it a little to get it all the way in her. Blood gushes from all around the stake. When I finally pierce her heart, she stops all movement and sound. Her eyes are still open and I think she can still see me. It must be horrible to be trapped, fully aware and able to see but not able to move at all. I wonder if she can still feel the intense pain of her burnt flesh but cannot even scream.

"Becket, god damnit, report," Agent Smith yells into my ear.

"I am at the upstairs bathroom. I managed to stake Tina. Two Hounds have been killed," I report into my mic.

"Good job. We will come to you. The helicopter from HEL should be here in twenty," Agent Smith informs.

The helicopter will be carrying Bravo team. HEL should have been monitoring everything that has happened here. I pick up the Hound's Blaster and check to make sure it has a full charge. I back into the bathroom and point the blaster at the open doorway. The hair on the back of my neck starts to stand up and I know something bad is going to happen.

I can see all of Tina's body except for her legs from where I am crouching down at in the bathroom. Suddenly Tina's body is jerked out of my view.

"Contact. They are taking Tina's body," I report as I leap into the hall. I see Lilly leaning over Tina crying. She is still holding her dolly. I almost feel sorry for Lilly. It must have been horrible for her to see her mother murdered and then turned into a vampire when she was six. A hundred years later and she is still looking for a mother to replace her lost one. No matter what she has been through, she is now a monster and must be put down I tell myself as I pull the trigger on my Blaster. Flame engulfs Lilly as she pulls the stake out of Tina.

I see Lilly move to shield her doll from the fire. She is allowing herself to be bathed in fire rather than have the one thing her mother gave her be hurt. Lilly smashes through a bedroom door and drags Tina with her. I let go the trigger on the Blaster so I can follow Lilly. I get to the bedroom doorway and watch as Lilly tosses Tina through the second story window breaking it all to pieces. Lilly's back is charred and most of her beautiful hair is burnt off. She turns to me and I can see hate in her eyes. I'm stunned when the hate instantly turns to loving innocence.

"Come with us, Mommy," Lilly pleads, as she reaches her little hand out to me.

I pull the trigger on my Blaster to answer her with a jet of flame. Lilly turns and leaps out the window before the fire reaches her. My blast sets part of the room on fire but I do not care. I go to the window and pull out my pistol. I shoot into Tina's unmoving body as Lilly pulls it away from the house through the tall grass.

Agent Smith and one of the Hounds come in the room behind me. They are too late to see Tina being drug away by Lilly. They help me put out the fire in the room.

We hole up in the bedroom until the helicopter gets here. Bravo team sweeps the area. A trail is found where Lilly dragged Tina's body away. The decision is made that we should follow. The helicopter takes off to fly support. Team Bravo, Agent Smith, our remaining Hound and I all follow Lilly and Tina into the woods.

At first, we move quickly but soon the undergrowth becomes too thick. We walk for over two miles before we find Tina's body. She is dead. Her body has changed. She has decomposed to a corpse a couple years old. Some of the Hounds bag and tag the body and bring it along. Lilly's tracks disappear so we head back to the house.

The house is swept. Bravo team is left to handle cleanup while Agent Smith and myself fly back to HEL for debriefing.

Chapter Fourteen: Debriefing

Our debriefing is intense and takes over three hours. Three different people who mostly ask the same questions interview me. I know all the footage and our statements will be gone over by a team of analysts before a report will ever be written. Nevertheless, I still have to write my own report of what happened. I am beat by the time the debrief is over so I crash in bed.

The next day I attend an after mission meeting in the conference room. Director Palmer is presiding over the meeting personally. Agent Smith, Frank from research and Dr. Brad Hasty are also in attendance. Assistant Director Carver attends through video conference.

"First I would like to take a moment to remember the four brave men that were killed during this mission. Next, I would like to commend Agent Smith and Becket for their courage under extraordinary circumstances. Becket showed considerable skill and kept a level head on her first mission. She will receive a personal commendation in her official file from me and Agent Smith," Palmer comments looking at me approvingly.

"The body found in the woods was indeed Tina Wilson's. Dr. Hasty will tell us more about it," Palmer says.

"Tina Wilson's body decomposed to what it would have looked like if it had been in a sealed room away from bugs for just over two years. This and other unsubstantiated evidence up until now lead us to believe that a vampire's body ages at the time of final death to what it was when it was made into a vampire. In Mrs. Wilson's case, she was made a vampire just over two years ago, so her body aged to then. A few old files speak of this happening in other cases. One body with several eyewitnesses reports the death of a vampire reverting to a centuries old skeleton. This is an exciting breakthrough to have physical evidence to support this theory," Brad reveals.

"We were, however, unable to get any good blood samples or physical evidence at all that Tina Wilson was a vampire. This is consistent with other cases we have on file. It seems that at time of final death all the blood is decomposed with the body and returns to its human form. All other tissue and bone also revert to its original human nature," Brad continues.

"There were several wounds that were still present on Tina Wilson's body when recovered. Much of the fire damage was unhealed but there were signs that it was healing. There are several bullet wounds including a couple that were caused post-mortem,"

Brad says looking at me smiling. "From going over the reports about the encounter with Tina Wilson it seems that vampires can use blood to heal themselves. They can expel bullets from their body and fully heal the wounds. They seem to be able to even heal burns with fresh blood. Becket, I want to thank you for your very detailed description of how it all happened in the field."

Palmer clears his throat and then begins to speak. "The mission was only a partial success. Even though Becket managed to stake Mrs. Wilson, her accomplice Lilly was able to remove the stake and get away. I commend you for killing a vampire but we should have done better. I know that we are all disappointed at how little the new HEIAP ammo did. I promise you we will rework the mixture on the ammo and have a new batch for testing soon."

"Everyone agrees that Lilly is pursuing you, Becket. This means she may come here. Security will be heightened for at least the next six months. There is a possibility Lilly will be unable to track you here or will give up but we are going to proceed as if she is still hunting you. You will go to and from Rolla by helicopter and only once a month from now on. You will not be allowed off base without an escort or partner. Lilly is a very old and persistent hunter. We will do what we can to protect you, Becket," Director Palmer states.

The rest of the meeting is about things more trivial. My mind drifts to thoughts of Lilly anyway. I knew she was hunting me but now I have killed her companion. I am sure I will see Lilly again. I believe the next time I fight Lilly only one of us will walk away.

Chapter Fifteen:
Lilly's Game

The next day Agent Smith comes to my room to talk to me. "Bravo team went back to the safe house for another sweep and to fully clean it. They found numbers painted in the house over where each Hound was killed. The numbers were 8, 9, 10 and 11. They were all drawn in blood by a child's size finger. I thought you would want to know," Agent Smith informs.

"She went back and drew the numbers? They must really be important to her. On the other hand, maybe they are for me. I am the only other living person that was there when the first number was drawn. I think the numbers are for me to see. She is keeping track of the ones she kills until she gets to me," I realize, getting a chill that runs up my spine.

"I think the numbers are for both you and Lilly. She is playing a game with you and keeping score," Agent Smith admits.

"We should go back to where we found Tina's body and mark a 1 on the ground. I bet Lilly will find it and follow my trail. We could intentionally lead her into another trap."

"That is pretty sick but it just might work. Get ready to go. I will clear it with Palmer," Agent Smith orders as he walks out of my room.

I'm ready to go by the time Agent Smith comes to get me. We travel by helicopter and are taken to the safe house while there is still daylight with four heavily armed Hounds. We locate the spot we found Tina. I build a large number 1 in the ground out of rocks. The Hounds start to help but I tell them I should do this alone for it will mean more to Lilly. Afterwards we go back to the house and get in an SUV that was brought for us. I make sure I touch lots of grass and trees on the way to the vehicle to leave my scent.

We drive an hour away to another safe house. I spend an hour walking around leaving my scent as the Hounds set the house up with cameras and motion sensors. Agent Smith and I fly back from this second safe house in the Helicopter. Bravo team remains onsite to watch for Lilly.

On the way to my first rotation at the second safe house, we stop at the first safe house to check on the number one I left next to where we found Tina's body. The stones have been violently scattered all around. None of the stones remains where I placed them. I know I got to Lilly.

My rotation at the second safe house goes uneventfully and I return to HEL for more training. I continue with my training but I can see it will soon come to an end. I am able to spend the weekend with Brian, and am renewed by just being with him. He knows something is wrong and keeps asking me about it. Saturday night after a few glasses of wine I feel relaxed enough to talk to him.

"I know you are worried about me. I don't want to burden you with my problems but I think you really want to know. Am I right?" I ask Brian as I sit next to him on the couch.

"I need to know. I'm here away from you most of the time and it's kind of driving me crazy. When you got here last night, you were different. What has happened to you? I need to be part of your life as much as I can," Brian pleads.

"I know Brian. I'll tell you," I hesitate, refilling my glass, as I figure I will need it.

"Last week we set a trap for the mass murderer from the Goodrest Ranch. I was present when our trap was sprung. The only problem is the mass murderer ambushed us. She had an apprentice with her. We lost four heavily armed men. Two of them died right in front of me. I managed to kill the apprentice murderer but the true master is still free. I know she is still hunting me," I confess, remembering the horrific events.

"Oh my God, honey. How can you...I had no idea. You could have been killed," Brian gasps, leaning close to me and hugging me.

"It is my job. We will never truly be safe until the murderer is captured or killed. It was horrible. I hate that good men died. But it had to be done," I say hugging Brian back.

193

"Do you think we are safe here?" Brian breathes, looking around the house.

"I'm really sorry I have brought all this danger and lies into your life. I hope you don't regret your decision to be with me." My eyes start to well up in tears. "I think we are safe for now. We may one day have to move if I cannot capture the one hunting me," I admit.

"I want to be with you come what may, Becket. You will get your man and we will go back to a more normal life. Until then, we will take what time we can get together. I fall you and I love you Becket," Brian vows kissing me.

I hear what Brian is saying but I know things are changing between us. He is not nearly as full of life as he was. He is apprehensive all the time. Conversation is over now as Brian is kissing me. I try to forget Lilly and just enjoy being loved by Brian. I drift off to sleep with Brian's arms around me.

…..

I see Lilly watching the second safe house. She creeps around the house until she sees a Hound leaning close to a window. She reaches up putting her hand right through the window grabbing the Hound. She pulls him out the window and feasts on his blood. She rips off his head and gouges out his eyes. Her dolly seems to talk to her and she makes it dance over the eyes. She puts his eyes in a drawstring bag to keep. She draws the number 12 on the side of the house in his blood before moving off. She creeps around the house. I can see her watching Easley and LeClerc talking. They are on high alert and know they have a man down. Lilly leaps to the second floor roof from the ground. She moves to an upstairs window and goes inside the house. She goes into the hall and is shot three times before she brings down another Hound. She feasts on him drinking his blood. I watch as the three still burning bullets are expelled from her body and healed over. She grabs his head, twists, and snaps it off. She takes his eyes and shows them to her dolly before putting them in her bag. She draws a number 13 on the wall next to the fallen Hound, using his own blood.

Lilly next makes her way down the hallway and finds another Hound. The Hounds lets Lilly have it with his Blaster. Lilly screams and moves incredibly fast to get through the flames and at the Hounds back. She tears at his neck ripping it from his body. She drinks from him as the still activated Blaster sets the room on fire. She takes his eyes and puts them in her bag. Lilly then draws a number 14 on the wall in blood before going out the window. The house is burning down around us.

Lilly drops to the ground and walks around the house. She watches as the men inside see the house is on fire. Easley, LeClerc and the two remaining Hounds make a break for it out the front door to one of the SUVs. Lilly is waiting for this and comes up behind them picking off a straggling Hound. She rips off his head and drinks from him. The others get in the SUV and drive away. Lilly plucks out his eyes and gently places them in her bag. I watch as Lilly draws a 15 in the dirt and fills it with blood.

It is as if I am inside the number 15 drawn in the earth as blood comes up all around me. I claw at the earth trying to get out but it is no use. I fall into the blood and am drowning. I awake screaming, shaking and covered in sweat. Brian is looking at me in horror. I get out of bed and grab my phone. I go to the bathroom and lock the door. I call Agent Smith.

"Hello?" Answers a very much awake Agent Smith even though it is the middle of the night.

"Lilly has attacked Bravo team. The safe house is on fire and only Easley, LeClerc and one of the Hounds got away in an SUV," I pant, breathing hard.

"I am just coming into the conference room now. I will get back to you when I know more," Agent Smith vows as he disconnects.

I sit on the toilet holding the phone. A knock comes at the door.

"What is going on? Who are you talking to?" Brian probes through the door.

I open the door and hug Brian. "It is part of my nightmare therapy. I have to call in and report every time I have one. I'm sorry I didn't tell you. I don't have too many anymore," I lie to Brian as I continuing to hug him.

"What was it about?"

"People dying, a house burning and me drowning in blood. Fairly normal for me," I say, trying to make a joke but not really feeling it.

"That is horrible. Do you want to come back to bed?"

"I'm going to find something light hearted on TV to watch. It will help me forget my nightmare," I say before looking at Brian. "You once told me that as long as we love each other everything will be ok. Do you still believe that?"

"I want to but it has been really difficult this last month. I can't talk to my friends or family. I never even know if it is going to be you at the door or someone telling me you are dead," Brian admits.

I know Brian wants to talk but I just can't. Everything is so out of control and I don't know what to do next. I thought I could get the upper hand on Lilly but I was wrong. I am so afraid that by trying to keep Brian near me I am going to get him killed.

Brian and I watch some TV and fall asleep on the couch. My phone ringing wakes me. It is Agent Smith.

"The safe house burned down. There is no sign of Lilly. The rest is as you reported. All units are returning to base. You are to report back tonight as normal," Agent Smith says, and then disconnects.

I spend the rest of the day with Brian then go back to HEL by helicopter. I settle in at the HEL facility and complete my training over the next couple of weeks.

I'm paired with Agent Smith and given two weeks off to spend with Brian. When I return to work, Agent Smith and I will be given our first assignment. It feels good to have finally completed training.

Now that I am a full field Agent of HEL, I can think a little about what I would like to do. My thoughts always return to Lilly. I know Brian and I can never truly be safe until Lilly is dealt with. She is used to being the unchallenged hunter of Norms, hunting for a replacement for her mother and for blood. I used to be easy prey for her, just like any other Norm, but now, I have the training, support and weapons to become the hunter.

Chapter Sixteen:
Prey

I start my vacation with Brian in Rolla. I want to call my parents and arrange to visit them in Seattle over the weekend. This first night I want to spend with Brian alone. Even though he does not show it very much Brian is upset with me. I have pretty much ruined his life. I have been considering breaking it off, at least until this whole Lilly situation is dealt with. But I think it is too late for that, I think Lilly will hunt him if he is with me or not. Brian is unhappy even if he won't admit it. I just want to spend a night alone without any worries and then I will talk to him about going to Seattle with me.

Everything goes well. We don't talk about anything important and just enjoy being together. The doorbell ringing at 1 a.m. awaking me. I pull on my sweats but stop as I hear something, the sound "tap, tap, tap" is coming from outside. It speeds up. I realize it is keeping rhythm with the beating of my heart. The last time I heard something similar was at my Gran's house. But he could not be here, could he?

"What is wrong, Becket? You just froze. I think someone is at the door," Brian yawns, getting out of bed. Brian's voice brings me back to here and now. I can no longer hear the tapping sound. I finish putting my sweats on and get my gun. Brian looks at the gun and stops in his tracks. He just stares at me like, "What the hell are you doing?"

"It is too early for any girl scouts to be selling cookies. You stay here," I fake a grin to Brian.

Brian grabs my hand to keep me in the room but I pull away. I to need check this out. I walk to the door and look through the peephole. I don't see anything. I flick the locks and open the door. Just outside the door is a box. I look all around then flip on the light. The box has "Rebecca" written on the top.

Oh damn, I think to myself. The only people who know me as Rebecca are my family. I know this box is not from my parents so that just leaves my family from the old country. I pick up the box and go back inside.

"It's ok, Brian, it was just a package for me."

"OK, come back to bed."

"I'll be there in a minute," I say, examining the box. Opening the box, I see a hand knitted wool scarf. It looks like the ones my Gran used to make me. There is also a note.

"Dearest Rebecca, I had hoped that you would have come home by now. I have so many things I wish to talk to you about. One day we will have to make up for lost opportunities.

"You have become entangled in a very dangerous game. The little girl knows where you are and will be coming soon. I could help you get rid of her but I respect your wishes to make your own way in the

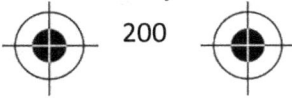

world. I surmise you thought what I offered you so long ago was a trapped life. How is the life you have chosen for yourself any less of a trap? At least with me you would have been with family.

"If you want my help, come out of your house now. I will protect you. If you choose to stand on your own, I wish you luck. Yours, A."

It only takes me a moment to make up my mind. I dial Agent Smith as I go to get my Blaster.

"What is it with you and the middle of the night?" a very sleepy sounding Agent Smith asks.

"Lilly is coming for me tonight. She is coming to my house," I stammer, not really knowing what to do.

"Hold on," Agent Smith says.

I get my Blaster out of the bedroom and see that Brian is asleep. I consider waking him but decide against it. I put an extra gun on the nightstand next to Brian just in case he needs it.

"Becket?" Agent Smith asks.

"Yes, I am here."

"Bravo team will be in the air in ten minutes. It will take them another twenty to get to you. Do you want to call in local police? Their presence might scare her off," Agent Smith questions.

"Yes. Call them in. I'm going to leave this line open to you. I'm switching to my mic."

"Good, I'm going to the conference room. I'll have your mic connected in there and routed to Bravo team. I am still here but am going to be multitasking."

I walk around the house checking windows and looking outside. At the side window, I see Lilly in the neighbor's swing with her doll. She is wearing the same kind of old fashion frilly dress as her dolly. She is just rocking herself back and forth in the swing brushing her doll's hair. She looks up at me and smiles. I turn to pull out my gun. Lilly is gone by the time I glance back. She is just so fast.

I hear the alarm warning go off that a window has been opened. I go to the alarm panel and see the red light is blinking next to the master bedroom window. Oh, my god, she is in the bedroom with Brian. I race to the bedroom and fling open the door. Lilly is sitting in bed next to Brian, who is still sleeping. Lilly is petting his hair and looking at him fondly.

"I like my new Daddy, Mommy. Dolly is happy to have a Daddy again," Lilly whispers, looking at Brian.

I'm not really sure what to say.

"I bet he has beautiful eyes like in his photo," Lilly sighs, petting Brian's hair.

"What do you want Lilly?" I ask quietly.

"I want us to be a family, Mommy. You, me, dolly and Daddy together forever," Lilly sighs gazing up at me. She looks so sweet right now that I almost believe her.

"We are a family," I lie, still pointing my gun at Lilly.

"I'm glad, Mommy," Lilly smiles while she pets Brian's hair.

I hear sirens and know that the regular police will be knocking on my door soon. I know Lilly hears them too.

"What did you do, Mommy? Did you call the bad people? I hate the way they all look at me," Lilly scowls.

I am not sure what to do but I need to stall for time. "Is that why you take their eyes?" I ask Lilly.

"Dolly says they think I'm a monster. All of them look at me with their horrible eyes. I can see myself through their eyes. I hate when they look at me," Lilly hisses.

The sirens are about at the house and Brian is beginning to wake up.

"We should go, Mommy. The bad men are coming," Lilly pleads.

"What bad men?" Brian yawns.

Lilly turns to Brian and I take a chance.

"BANG, BANG, BANG..." I unload my gun into Lilly's back.

Lilly leaps across Brian and out the open window. I move to the window and reload my weapon.

"Brian get the gun on the nightstand and lock yourself in the bathroom," I command.

When Brian does not move I grab him and lead him into the bathroom. "Lock the door, I will be back," I say, as I hand Brian a gun and pull the door shut.

"Aaahhh," I hear coming from the front of the house.

I grab my Blaster and head for the front door.

"Becket, stay in the house," Agent Smith orders through my mic.

"She is killing cops," I insist, as I run out the door.

I see Lilly rip the head off a cop and another one lying in the street missing his head. I close on Lilly and let her have it with my Blaster. Jets of flame pour over her. I am nearly overwhelmed by the toxic smell of burnt flesh and hair. At such close range, the heat generated by the fire is stifling.

Lilly grabs the Blaster in my hands and wrenches it around at me.

"AAAHHH!!!" I scream.

I have never felt such pain. It is my flesh, my hair that is burning now. I pass out.

Sometime later, I start to regain consciousness. I hear Lilly talking. "I hate the way you looked at me, Mommy," I hear Lilly saying.

I hurt all over. It even hurts to breath. I open my eyes. I see Lilly kneeling beside me with her knife. The same knife she uses to cut people's eyes out. I try to fight her but I'm too badly burned. I watch as she brings the knife right to my eye. Then, all there is, is PAIN!

"AAAHHH!!!" I scream.

As I am slipping out of consciousness, I hear a faint tapping sound before I black out.

Chapter Seventeen: Aftermath

I awake in a seedy hotel room. I'm wearing clothes I never owned. None of my stuff is in the room. I'm very hungry. I feel as if I haven't eaten in weeks. I look at myself in the mirror. I'm not burned at all and I have both eyes. What the hell happened to me?

The stationary reads Rolla Rocky Inn. I pick up the phone and dial Brian's house but the number has been disconnected. I call Agent Smith.

"Yes," Agent Smith says.

"This is Becket."

"Becket? Is that really you Becket?" Agent Smith questions.

"Yes. What is going on? I just woke up in a hotel room."

"What is the last thing you remember?"

"Lilly cutting my eye out with her knife. But I have both eyes," I admit, feeling my face just to make sure.

"Where are you?" Agent Smith demands.

"The Rolla Rocky Inn."

"Stay right there I will be there as soon as I can. It will be about thirty minutes."

"Ok, I will wait," I reply, not understanding what happened to me.

I look around the room and try to remember how I got here. Even my underwear is not mine. Someone dressed me. I decide to call the front desk.

"Rolla Rocky Inn, where you can rock by the hour. How may I help you?" the voice mumbles.

"When do I have to check out?" I ask.

"Your room is paid up for another four days. You must be having yourself quite a party," the clerk teases snickering.

"We paid in cash, right?" I ask hoping the answer will be no.

"Yep, all paid up in cash. If you want to watch the dirty movies you have to give me a credit card," the clerk warns.

"Do you have room service?" I wonder since I am so hungry.

"Hahaha…you mean like edible panties or flavored condoms? We got those in the office but we don't deliver anymore," the clerk chuckles.

"Thanks for the info," I say and I hang up.

The thirty minutes pass slowly. But soon Agent Smith is knocking at my door. I open the door and Agent Smith walks in. He checks out the room, inspecting everything.

"Grab the key and let's go," Agent Smith orders.

I do as I'm told and follow Agent Smith out to his car. It's a rental. We drive out of town without talking. He pulls down a side road and gets out the security wands. I go along with it but cannot imagine

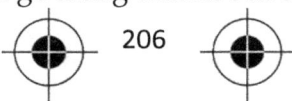

what the hell is going on. When he is satisfied I am not bugged, we get back in the car and he looks at me.

"Where have you been?" Agent Smith inquires.

"Um, I told you the last thing I remember is being at Brian's house fighting Lilly. She turned the Blaster on me. I thought she cut out one of my eyes. I just now woke up in that seedy hotel. I'm wearing clothes that I don't recognize. What the hell is going on?" I demand, starting to get pissed.

"You have been missing since that night when you encountered Lilly. That was forty-six days ago. We thought Lilly had killed or turned you into a vampire," Agent Smith says.

"What? A month and a half. That is crazy."

"Yes, it is crazy, but it is the truth. Do you have any idea what happened to you?"

"No idea. Wait, where is Brian? Does he think I'm dead?"

"Brian has been missing since the same night you disappeared."

"Damn it! Lilly got away, right?" I ask, unable to deal with Brian's disappearance yet.

"Lilly has not been seen since that night either. Is there anything else you can remember?" Agent Smith asks.

"Antal, I think it was Antal Degano who warned me Lilly was going to attack. He offered to help me, but I chose to call you instead. I think Antal might have saved me from Lilly."

"Really, Antal told you about Lilly?" Agent Smith asks me, somewhat amazed.

"I got a package from him right before I called you. It had a note in it warning me that Lilly was coming. It also had a scarf in it."

"Let's go to Brian's house and see if the note is still there," Agent Smith says.

We drive back to the house in Rolla. I'm startled when I see the police tape on the door. Of course, this is a crime scene but seeing it in person really brings it home. I was happy here with Brian and now that is over. We were both taken that night when Lilly attacked. I have been returned, healed from life-threatening wounds. Brian is still lost, maybe dead. I'm thinking so hard that I do not even notice we have parked until Agent Smith shuts his car door. I see him watching me as I snap out of it and follow him to the house.

The house looks pretty much the same. I see the box from Antal on the table but ignore it. I go back to the bedroom. I see the bathroom door has been smashed in and has bullet holes through it that were fired from the inside out. Someone broke down that door to get to Brian while he shot at them. It was probably Lilly or Antal. I wonder if I will ever know. Then I get an idea. I walk up to the bathroom door and put my hands on it and the door handle.

I fall into the vision of the door. I see a couple I do not know having sex up against the door, they are full

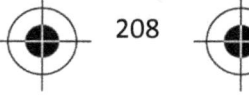

of lust and love. I see the woman from the couple leaning up against the door crying, she is much older and grieving. I see Lilly smashing down the door full of rage. I see Brian lean on the door handle as he is being led away by Lilly. Brian is afraid and confused.

I emerge from the vision. Agent Smith is standing beside me, waiting.

"I saw Lilly take Brian from the bathroom. He is probably dead," I declare. The realness of Brian's fate starts to sink into me. "This is all my fault. If I had kept Brian out of this, he would still be alive. I was selfish to try to cling to Brian's love. I'm going to kill Lilly the next time I see her."

I walk back into the kitchen and look on the table. I open the box, the scarf and note are all still inside. I pick up the scarf and let the vision envelop me. I see my grandmother making the scarf, filled with her love for me. I see Gran putting the scarf in the box, she is filled with hope and love.

I come out of the vision and pick up the note from Antal. I let the vision of the note wash over me.

I see Antal writing the note but I cannot read his emotions. I see him put the note into the box with the scarf but still no emotions. I see myself in the box as it starts to fill up with blood. I begin to drown in the blood. Then something strange happens. A hand grabs me and pulls me out of the blood. I see Antal standing before me. He has saved me from drowning. We are standing together with darkness all around.

"I had hoped you would use your gifts on the note when you discovered it, or walked outside for my protection. You are a very special girl who should not be so anxious to throw away your life," Antal states matter of factly.

"Is this really happening? Are you in my vision now or is this a reflection of you?" I ask.

"I fashioned the note so I could talk to you privately when you used your gift upon it. It might be overly dramatic but I did not think I would be welcomed for dinner," Antal explains.

"What do you want?"

"I want you to live. I hope you will choose to come home to your family where you belong."

"I remember Lilly burning me and hurting me. What happened after that?" I inquire.

"I drove Lilly away and carried you to safety. I healed your wounds as best I could. Then I let you go to make your own decisions," Antal confesses.

"So you left me in that hotel?"

"Yes. I know it was not the nicest place but they did not ask any questions. I knew you would awaken soon," Antal admits.

"What about Brian? Where is he?"

"I do not know. You were near death and I had to act immediately to save you," Antal apologizes.

"Lilly took Brian."

"Lilly will not hunt you again. You are free of her. It is my gift to you," Antal informs.

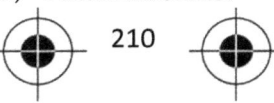

"So you just told her to leave me alone and she agreed?"

"Something like that."

"What about Brian?" I ask.

"Brian is either dead, a slave to Lilly or has been turned. In any event, he is lost to you."

"You mean turned into a vampire? Are you a vampire?"

"Yes, I meant turned into a vampire. I do not wish to answer your other question directly. Let us just say I am a concerned member of your family."

"So you want me to move to Degano Valley and work for you?"

"Your grandmother and I would like that very much. I feel you have misjudged us. I know you love your grandmother. If you had not met that little child hellion, you most likely would have come to us on your own by now."

"What kind of work would I do with you and Gran?"

"Our family is large, so there are many different things you could do including things similar to what you are doing here. It would be up to you. I will not force you to come home but I hope you will," Antal assures.

"I'm young and have not really given this job a chance. My life has been defined for a couple of years now by that night I met Lilly. I have been trapped by the constant threat of her jumping out of a shadow. I need time to adjust, to see what else is out there," I say, still in shock from all that has happened.

"I understand and would expect nothing less from you. I am very proud of you Rebecca. I will be here if you need me. I wish you long life and good fortune," Antal smiles as the vision fades.

I am back in the kitchen with Agent Smith.

"I am glad you are back, I was starting to get worried," Agent Smith says.

"How long was I holding the note?"

"Ten minutes. You only touched the scarf and door for about 10 seconds each."

"Antal wants me to go home to my family in Italy and work with him. He saved me from Lilly and has arranged it so she will not hunt me anymore," I explained.

"I will not stop you if you want to go to Antal. You know that HEL will mark you as a threat and you will be watched. I do not think HEL would ever move against you in Italy but if you travel, you might be contacted or captured for interrogation," Agent Smith tells me.

"I'm going to stay in HEL for now. Brian might still be alive. I need to know what happened to him. Someday I may go home to see Antal, but who knows if I'll stay. Let me grab some stuff and then we can go back to HEL."

I know I need to mourn Brian, but I just can't. I have to hold on to the hope that he is out there

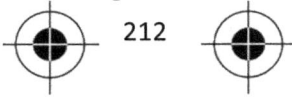

somewhere and I can save him. The day I lose that hope, I will lose a part of myself. I am so sorry, Brian. I love you, wherever you are.

Now it is time to rest and regroup for what lies ahead. This is not the end, just the beginning of my Eternal Hunt.

Savage Summer

Vampire
Rock and Roll

Lucas McWilliams

Savage Summer

Set in contemporary Seattle, *SAVAGE SUMMER* is a YA novel that is a supernatural thriller as well as a love story.

Seventeen-year-old Duncan is pretty sure he died recently in the car crash that killed his foster mother. His life really gets complicated when he is thrust into a new foster home, a new high school, falls in love with Amber, the hottest redhead in school, joins her rock band Savage Summer and develops a disturbing thirst for blood.

The band, Savage Summer, gets a gig at a local club, Eros, which turns out to be a haven for vampires. Duncan is forced to protect his new girlfriend Amber and the rest of the band from hungry bloodsuckers and the seductive tunes of Zeal, the vampire rock star.

Meanwhile the ruler of the city's vampires, Sapphire, is trying to seduce Duncan. But all Duncan is really interested in is trying to be a normal kid who feels he has finally found a family with Amber and Savage Summer. Duncan struggles with his love for Amber versus the realization she might be safer if he just walked away.

Preview of
Savage Summer
By Lucas McWilliams

Prologue

I have followed the light into darkness and been reborn in blood. The bright headlights of the murderous drunk driver's car that killed my foster mother and me. The darkness of Death that took me into his arms. The blood of my mother in my mouth invigorating every cell of my being. I woke out of death's embrace broken and battered beside my lifeless mother. I got into the car just a normal kid, but I crawled away from the wreckage somehow changed.

Chapter One:
First Day

Two weeks ago, my foster mother Tammy died in a car wreck, hit by a drunk driver. I was in the car with her when a stupid drunk kid plowed into us. He died instantly, so did Tammy. The crazy thing is, I'm pretty sure I died as well. Today, I start over again at a new school with a new set of foster parents.

Soon I'll be forced to walk the gauntlet again. I try to prepare myself for the barrage of assaults my senses will experience. Today would be bad enough if I was a local, but I'm an outsider once again, an easy target, the stranger no one knows. I've experienced first hand how my peers dread the new kid, fearing the possibility of losing their place in the pecking order. Today is my first day at a new school yet again.

School started a month ago so I'll stand out like a huge pimple on the end of a nose. If that is not enough, I just moved in with new foster parents. The Schwartz's seem nice but they sure are super old. Both of them have white hair and have to be in their late sixties. My Social Services caseworker commented that it was remarkable of them to take me for my junior year on such short notice. They do have the nicest house I've ever lived in.

If I can make it to the end of the school day, I'll be ok. I know each day after the first will get a little better. I can do this. I've been to three other schools in the last five years so one more, and they are all alike. I know the new kid routine, so being at this new school won't kill me.

I climb out of bed and get ready for school. I don't have much to wear. Mabel, or Mrs. Schwartz, said she would take me shopping for some new clothes but we haven't had time yet.

Until recently, I was living with Jim and Tammy Sloan down in Tacoma, WA. I had been with them for just over a year. They were not the nicest couple, but they treated me all right. Jim occasionally drank too much, but as long as I stayed out of his way, there was little trouble. He did hit me a couple of times, but I learned pretty quickly to not be around when he was drinking. He hit Tammy a few times and I did not like that at all. He never hurt her bad but I couldn't stand it.

About six months ago, Jim got piss drunk and really started in on Tammy. I tried to stop him and he turned his attention to me. I was black and blue for a week. I could've reported him to foster care but they just would have placed me somewhere new. I was tired of going from home to home and I had a few friends and a decent job. I worked as a mechanic at a motorcycle shop. It was not the most glamorous job but I was learning some stuff and making some pocket money. Probably the best thing it did was keep me busy so I couldn't get into too much trouble.

Living with the Sloans was the best I'd had it since my mom died when I was thirteen. When she died, I took it hard. It was just her and me. My dad left before I was born. I knew nothing about him until a month ago. I was going through some of my mom's old things and came across a note, she wrote about my father being in a rock band called the Night Wailers. His name was Jason Lust. Sounds more like a porn name than a rock star. I have enough things to worry about today without thinking about this. I try to calm myself down and put the images of the wreck out of my mind.

"Duncan, it's time for breakfast," Mabel calls from downstairs.

Mabel is in a fluffy pink housecoat when I get to the kitchen. I stop myself from laughing. Mabel is just a little thing around five feet tall with steel grey hair still bound up in curlers. She has a plate of scrambled eggs, toast and bacon ready for me.

"Thanks, Mabel. I'm not used to such a good breakfast," I say with a grin.

Mabel's husband Jerry is waiting in the car when I come out. Jerry looks like he's had a few too many beers in his life and they all went to his gut. He is a nice old coot who keeps to himself. He listens to talk radio as he drives me to school.

My new high school resembles something out of the future. It looks more like an all glass corporate building than a school. It is one of the top 20 high schools in the nation, which is a hell of a step up for me. This is Bellevue, WA where the rich live. We are a stone's throw from Microsoft. I've only been here a couple days and I have no idea where the poor people live around here. They must work the service jobs and commute in. On the roads all I see are shiny new Porsches, BMWs, Mercedes and huge SUVs.

I get my class list and locker. Already I can tell my clothes are all wrong. Great, just keep a low profile, Duncan. You can do this. Just seven hours and your first day will be over.

Math is the first class on the schedule. The teacher takes my "new kid" note and points to a seat in the back. Equations that look totally foreign to me fill the board and handouts I'm passed. I can tell I'm going to be in catch up mode for a long time.

As I try to find my next class, I ignore the stares and whispered comments about the new kid. In a school of over a thousand students, you would think I could just blend in, but I have always stood out in a crowd. My hair is jet black with a haircut my new foster parents call "edgy". My skin is very tan. My eyes don't really fit, registering the lightest blue. I have been told the whole package works. This and the fact that I am wearing second-hand ratty clothes makes me stick out.

I make it to lunch without any real incidents. In the cafeteria, the unthinkable happens. A pretty girl talks to me.

"Oh, you like the Pixies?" The gorgeous redhead in the lunch line behind me says.

It takes a minute to register she is talking to me.

"Your shirt, umm the Pixies? Do you like them?"

"Oh yeah, of course I like the Pixies. Who doesn't?" I lie.

This is one of my mom's old shirts that I keep around and wear every once in a while. Today I guess I wanted her strength with me. Now one of the hottest girls at school is making small talk with me about a band I have never even listened to and know nothing about.

"A lot of people have never heard of the late 80's punk bands. But the Pixies could really wail," she says as we work the line.

The food is better than any other school I have ever attended. I guess rich kids get better food as well as a better education.

"My mom gave me this shirt. She really liked the Pixies," I say, wishing I had not just mentioned my mom.

"Oh that's so cool. I wish my parents listened to music I could relate to. I think they only listen to people who are already dead. Or at least their music sounds that way...ha ha ha." Her eyes sparkle and crinkle at the edges when she laughs.

"Have you ever heard of Jason Lust?" I ask, trying to keep the conversation going.

"He was that local guy... rock legend from the late 90's. I've listened to a couple bootleg recordings and read a couple articles about him. His band was amazing. He died right before he made it to the mainstream. You know, now that I think about it you remind me of him."

I can't believe this girl has heard of my dad. Hell, she knows more about him than I do.

"He was my dad." I let drop, trying more to score points with her than being proud of it.

"Really, that's so cool! You're new here, right?"

"Yep. Today is my first day. Don't you notice that new kid smell?" I've found it helpful to try to make a joke in these situations before.

She smiles at me and I think I'm in love. Either God blessed her teeth or gave her a wonderful orthodontist. Either way, her smile is the most beautiful I have ever seen. She must have a line of guys waiting to date her.

"Come on, new guy, you can sit with me." She says, leading the way through the lunchroom.

I can see people's eyes on me as we walk. We go past the no man's land of rejects that are forced to sit next to the lunch line, through the layers of nerds and punks, on into the jocks and preps until we come to the promised land of the rich nestled by the huge windows in the back. I know this girl is way out of my league. But, I'm here, so I might as well give it a shot.

This elite area has small round tables for four. We walk deep into the rich zone right next to the windows. This means she has status even among them. We are the first two at the table. We sit and start to eat. I watch the stares from others trying to size me up. They are wondering what I'm doing in their space. I listen to their questioning whispers and smile to myself.

Ever since the car wreck, my senses have been alive. I can hear, smell, taste, see and touch with much more sensitivity. Like now when the lovely girl sitting next to me flips her hair. I can smell the jasmine shampoo she uses, mixed with her coconut body wash, combining and mingling with her natural girlie scent to create an intoxicating blend that defines her. I know I will be able to smell her in the hall, classrooms away.

"Do you ever go to any clubs?" The words bounce out between bites with ease.

"I just moved up here, but am looking forward to it," I reply. "Where should I go first?"

"Oh, Seattle is a great place for music. I'm in a band called Savage Summer. We have only played in public once but we're getting there. You'll have to come over and see us sometime. We practice at my house," she smiles at me.

"I'd love to. What instrument do you play?" I ask.

"I mostly sing but can play the guitar a little."

"I play guitar."

"Really? Are you any good?" She leans in closer to me.

I can see I hit the right chord with her. "I used to be pretty good, but I haven't played in a while. My mom taught me."

"You definitely have to come over now and audition. Maybe if you don't suck you can be in the band." She smiles and I grin back unable to stop myself.

"Cool, I'd love to give it a shot."

"Uh oh, - quick - what's your name?" She whispers, as she watches a tall guy beeline for our table.

"Duncan," I breathe.

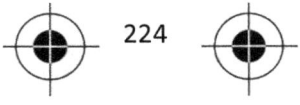

The tall guy walks up and sits on the other side of her. He leans over to kiss her but only gets the cheek. I can tell this pisses him off and all his fury is directed at me. He glares at me, eyes filled with contempt.

"Who's your new charity case, Amber?" The tall blond Abercrombie poster boy asks.

"Cody, Duncan. Duncan, Cody. He's trying out for the band." Amber's hand punctuates the introductions to first Cody, then me, then back again. Then her arm fell, patting me on the leg as she mentioned the band.

I watch Cody's eyes follow Amber's hand to my leg. My enhanced senses pick up how her fingers ever so slightly rub it as she raises her hand after every pat. It is subtle and maybe even unconscious but she is stroking my leg. I'm glad we are sitting down because I have definitely not learned how to control my enhanced senses. Amber's scent filling my head sends my teen hormones into overdrive. That mixed with her brilliant smile and leg stroking over-excites me.

I can tell Amber goes her own way. I like that in a girl. Hell, I like everything about this hot redhead. I bet she can wail into a microphone and make guys beg for more.

"Another wannabe I bet," Cody sneers, right before stuffing a hamburger in his mouth.

"I guess that's for Amber to decide," I stare at him, fixing him with an impatient glare.

225

Cody glares right back but has to chew his oversized bite before he can speak. Amber steps in before he has a chance to swallow.

"Play nice boys. Cody, Duncan is new to our school. We don't want him to get a bad impression on his very first day." Amber flashes another brilliant smile toward me.

I could just bask in her smile all day. She looks into my eyes and I melt. She has beautiful violet eyes. I've never seen anyone with such dramatic eyes, except for, maybe, myself. I can tell she is studying me, trying to figure out what makes me tick. Something catches her eye and she looks away. I follow her movement but am caught by Cody's glare. He has reason to be mad. I hope I'm stealing his girlfriend.

"Duncan, these are my friends. This is Taro Izumi and his better half, Taylor White," Amber says, causing me to snap out of my glaring war with Cody as she gestures towards the two new arrivals.

Taro is Japanese and looks to be a cool guy. All around the sides of his head, his jet-black hair is cut very short but the middle is long enough to flop to one side down to his ear. He helps Taylor into her chair and grabs another one from a nearby table.

"Hey guys, nice to meet you," I say, trying not to look as awkward as I feel.

"Pixies...huh, I can see why Amber picked you out. Welcome to the coolest table in the room." Taro chuckles, mostly laughing to himself.

"The coolest table in the room is wherever you are, right, baby?" Taylor obviously enjoys teasing Taro.

"You know it." Taro gives Taylor a good wet kiss.

"Duncan here is a guitarist. He's going to try out for the band," Amber says, looking at Taro.

"Really? That's great! I play drums, and lovely Taylor here plays the keyboard. Amber sings and strums a little," Taro says, obviously pumped about me being into music.

Taro was right about Taylor. She is lovely. She is downright hot, but obviously into Taro. She has soft blond hair that is long and full of curls. Her figure is fully formed in all the right places. I hope my string of good luck holds out long enough for me to get a permanent spot at this table and for that jackass Cody to get lost.

We finish lunch and Amber walks me out. "Give me your number so I can call you about the audition," Amber says as we walk.

"Give me a sec, it's here somewhere." I search my pockets. "Here it is." I hand her the only copy I have of my number.

She stops in the hall and punches it into her phone. She jots her number under mine and gives the slip of paper back to me.

"I'll call you after school. Can you come over around 4?" she asks.

"I'm pretty sure. I don't know my way around yet but I'll figure it out," I say.

"Where do you live? I'll just swing by and pick you up."

I rummage through my other pockets and hand her my address.

"K, got to run. I'll see you at 4, Duncan." Amber waves as she turns and walks down the hall.

I'm late to my next class. This draws unwanted attention but I'm so high from meeting Amber that I do not mind.

My next class is AP German. It is the only AP class I have this semester and frankly the only one I thought I could do. My mother spoke German and always pushed me to use it. Just speaking German reminds me of my mom. Whenever German is offered at a school, I make a point of taking it. I often study German on my own when I'm feeling alone in the world and want to remember how it was when it was just me and mom living together.

I have some trouble with all the proper sentence structure but am able to speak and read German very well. I hoped this would be an easy class but it looks like the teacher will push us harder than I expected. As my mind tries to focus on the teacher's German instructions, I find myself distracted by some whispering noises behind me.

 228

I always thought it would be cool to hear what people said to each other but I was wrong. I have to really concentrate to listen to the teacher and not all the little mini conversations going on between students. I have had enhanced senses since the crash but this is the first time I have found it so distracting and annoying.

Not only am I distracted by the other students' conversations, I start to feel hungry even though I just had lunch. I think it might be blood I am craving. It is the strangest thing but I can smell the slightest hint of blood in the air. It is so distracting in class when one of the girls smells of blood covered baby powder. I begin to wonder why I have started to notice the smell of blood around me when the bell rings, signaling the end of class. Wow! I am going to have to try to pay attention tomorrow because I can't remember what the teacher was telling us.

My last class of the day is art which I know I will enjoy, being the creative type. This semester is about different kinds of sculpture. Right now, the class is working with clay.

I am pleasantly surprised to see Amber walk into the room. She comes over.

"Hi stranger, mind if I sit with you?" Amber smirks jokingly, as she sits down.

"You are welcome by my side, fair lady." I play act as if I am tipping an imaginary hat.

"It is so nice to meet a gentleman," she smiles. For the first time, I notice the few cute freckles on her nose and cheeks as I return her smile.

She reaches into a shelf and shows me a house I figure she has been working on.

"What do you think?" she questions.

It is horrible. The roof is slanted and almost falling in and the sides are not even. It looks like it may fall down any moment.

"It should be condemned," I say, maybe being too honest.

"Ha ha ha...you are so right. That's Cody's house...ha ha ha. I think he only took art because I did. He is hopeless," Amber laughs.

"Wow, I'm glad it wasn't yours. I was a little harsh."

"Nah, you were so right. Anyway, I want my friends to be honest with me. So many people just say what they think I want to hear. It's refreshing to hear the truth, even if it is harsh." Amber says, pulling out a great sculpture of a castle that I can tell is hers.

"You're in my spot," Cody scowls, walking up.

"Is this Cody's spot, Amber?" I ask.

Amber gets up and walks around me looking at my chair. "No name on it so I guess not," Amber smirks, sitting back down next to me.

The rest of our table is full. I can see Cody eyeing the others and I know he considers making them move. He then catches Amber's annoyed expression

and thinks better of it. He takes his crappy house and sits at another table.

Amber and I joke during class. She notices I am good at art and I can tell she likes that. When class is over, we go our separate ways, but not before she reminds me she will pick me up at 4 . I watch Cody hook up with her and they walk off together. As they turn the corner Cody glares back at me and a grin fills his face. Day one is over and it was a pretty good day after all, despite all of the glares I got from that irritating Cody.

Jerry picks me up at school. He is listening to classical music and is pretty embarrassing in his lime green old people mobile. I don't totally dislike classical, but it can sometimes kind of put me to sleep. I know Jerry doesn't talk much but I need to know about meeting Amber.

"Hey Jerry, can I go over to a friend's house around 4?" I ask.

"You should ask Mabel, I don't know what she has planned," Jerry says.

"Ok. Thanks for picking me up from school," I say, trying to be nice.

"No problem, it was on my way from the center," Jerry says, meaning the senior center.

Jerry and Mabel are going to take some getting used to. I had an old beat-up car I could sometimes use when I lived with the Sloans but it looks like I am going to be at Jerry's mercy for now.

When I get home, I talk to Mabel.

"Is it cool if I go over to a friend's house around 4?" I ask, crossing my fingers.

"I was going to take you shopping for some new clothes," she hesitates as my eyes involuntarily dart to my shoes. "But I can see by your face you really want to go. We can go shopping some other time. Will you be home for dinner at 6?" Mabel inquires.

"I don't know, but probably not," I say, kind of hoping I'll be home late.

"Ok. Well, make sure you get something to eat. Do you need any money?" Mabel asks.

"I could use a little, that would be great." I say, thinking Mabel is all right.

"Here you go. Be home by 10. Is that ok?" Mabel says, giving me a twenty.

"Yea thanks, twenty will be great." I pocket the money.

"No, I meant is it ok for you to be home by 10?" Mabel asks.

I'm totally not used to a parent asking what time I should be home by. "10 should be good for a school night. Thanks for everything," I add, really meaning it.

Mabel tries to give me a hug and I don't know what to do. I just go with it and it feels kind of good. I know Mabel liked it. It is easier for me to think of Mabel and Jerry as grandparents.

I go to my room and look up some guitar music online. I also download some Pixies songs and put them on in the background. I don't own a guitar anymore so I hope Amber will let me use hers. I play air guitar to the music and am glad to find I still remember what my mother taught me.

Chapter Two:
Audition

Promptly at 4, a vibrant red Mercedes convertible with the top down pulls into my driveway. Amber is driving and Taro and Taylor are in the back seat. I head out of the house as they pull up so I don't have to deal with the whole foster parent thing.

I hop in the car.

"Where is your guitar?" Taro asks.

"I said I could play a guitar, not that I had one," I say, feeling embarrassed.

"Ha ha ha…yep. That's what you said. It's cool. You can use one of mine," Amber smiles patting me on the knee sending shivers up my spine. I try to think of the most unsexy thing I can to calm myself. I close my eyes and I remember the vision of Mabel in her green mud mask, neon blue curlers and pink nightgown from the night before. This fills me with enough revulsion to counteract even the lovely Amber's attentions.

We drive down by Lake Sammamish, which I can barely see from my house. Amber pulls into a gated driveway towards the lake. She enters a code and the metal gate slides out of the way. The house is gigantic, as are the grounds. They must own at least five lots. We drive by the main house and pull in front of a lakefront clubhouse. I can see there is also a beautiful two-story dock with at least three boats and jet skis. Man, this place is amazing.

"Welcome to the home of Savage Summer," Amber chimes as we walk in the clubhouse.

It is as big as the house I lived in with the Sloans. Most of the area is a great room with a bar, lots of comfortable chairs, a fireplace, stereo and TV. The back part of the room has been set up into a practice area for the band. It is a totally cool place just to hang out. Amber tells me that there are bathrooms and a kitchen through a door in the back.

"Take your pick of which guitar you would like to try. Take your time while we warm up," Amber says, pointing to a selection of guitars in a rack.

I find a rockin' Fender guitar that has to be worth a pretty penny. I plug it into an amp and give it a shot. It is sweet sounding, much better than anything I have ever played before. It takes me a few minutes to get used to it before I try any chords. My fingers welcome holding a pick again and all my lessons come flowing back. My new heightened senses give me even more control and clarity as I play. I can hear slight variations in how I am playing a particular chord and my touch is so acute that I can control what sounds vibrate forth much better. Soon I lose myself playing some old punk tunes my mom loved. After I'm done, I just enjoy the stillness until it is interrupted.

"Clap, clap, clap…" Amber, Taro and Taylor are applauding and staring at me amazed.

Taro has his mouth open in total surprise. "Damn that was awesome, dude. You have to join the band," Taro insists, almost jumping up and down.

"Sure, if it's cool with everyone," I say, looking to Amber.

"Welcome to Savage Summer, Duncan. Let's see how you do with some of our songs." Amber hands me some music.

I glance at the music. I give it a couple tries and I'm ready. So I really play it—all out. I know I am much better than I used to be. My new senses just bring the music alive within me and then I convey it through the guitar. I'm so totally caught up in the expression of the music that everything else seems to disappear. Once again, I come out of my trance to clapping.

"Wow, in like twenty minutes you played that better than anyone ever has. Amber, you found a keeper in this one," Taro exclaims, coming up and rubbing Amber on the shoulder.

"You are full of surprises, new kid," Amber jokes.

"Ok let's do it together. One, two, three…" Amber sings out as we all start playing.

We play song after song for the next three hours. We break for dinner when pizza arrives. A well-dressed man in his fifties brings our pizza in. I am sure he cannot be the pizza guy.

"Ms. Nobel, your pizzas have arrived. Will there be anything else?" the butler asks.

"No that's all Buckley. Thanks," Amber tossed over her shoulder as she reaches for some pizza.

"Help yourself everyone, we deserve a break after that great jam. There are drinks in the fridge," Amber says.

"Thanks for dinner," I say, munching on a slice of pepperoni.

"Thanks for not sucking," Amber smiles. "We have had a terrible time getting anyone who didn't suck on guitar. Most kids feel if they can score big on one with colored buttons they should be able to play one with strings."

"Ha ha ha...I suck at those games," I say. "But I'm really glad you gave me a chance. I've missed playing a real guitar."

"Well you are in now. I'm not going to let you get away." Again Amber's face lights up with one of those wonderful smiles.

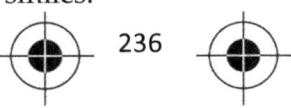

236

"I'm not going anywhere," I smile right back at her.

We finish dinner and play a couple more songs. Taro and Taylor leave around 8:30. I am alone with Amber and I can feel the tension in the air. This sounds crazy but I can smell that she likes me. I don't want to push too hard but I want her to know that I want to be more than friends.

We sit on the couch listening to music. I want to kiss her but am not sure. Damn, why do these things have to be so complicated? I like her and I can tell she likes me.

"So what's up with you and Cody?" I ask, just trying to break the silence.

"Well, he thinks he's my boyfriend." Amber's violet eyes sparkle in the dimming light.

"So you don't have a boyfriend?"

"Not yet, but I've my eye on this new guy," she smiles at me.

"He sure is a lucky guy." I mean every word.

"I think I should get to know him a little better before I decide." She teases me.

"So what would you want to know about this potential boyfriend?"

"Oh like, where he is from? What are his hobbies? Is he a good kisser? You know, normal stuff like that," she grins at me.

"Well I guess he might say he was born in Seattle but most recently moved from Tacoma. He likes playing guitar with his killer new band. Listening to music and doing art. But for the last thing, I think they would just have to give it a try," I smile as I lean over and kiss her.

It is ecstasy to kiss Amber. At first, our lips barely touch and gently rub against one another. Then she presses harder and our mouths become one. Her tongue darts in my mouth searching for mine and they do an erotic dance together. My senses are overwhelmed with her jasmine, coconut body wash mixed with her scent of arousal. This only enhances the kiss. My arms go around her, gently caressing her back. My hand glides up her back and skillfully plays with her neck and hair. I know our kiss only lasted a minute but it was more thrilling than I could imagine.

We rest in each other's arms. We hold each other, sharing this moment. The only movement is the flutter of our chests as we breathe. I feel and hear her heart beat. I can even hear the hot blood running through her veins. So alive and so beautiful. The sounds of her breathing and blood pumping fill my ears even over the music playing in the background. It is nice to sit in stillness with her.

After several minutes, Amber breaks the silence. "I'm glad we met today. We were floundering without a good guitarist," Amber whispers to me.

"So you just like me for my big guitar? I see how it is," I tease her.

"I thought you didn't even have a guitar, let alone a big one," Amber teases me back.

Then she kisses me. It is like our first kiss, but even better. We are not as afraid of rejection. We are freer to experiment. Her lips move beyond my lips to my cheek and neck, then up to my ear. I feel her breath caressing my skin and sensitive hairs on my neck. Shivers run down my spine as I follow her lead and kiss her neck and ear. I tempt fate by moving beyond my lips, to using teeth to nibble here and there. The sound of her blood flowing right under my mouth calls to me. I can even feel the blood pumping through her veins with my tongue. I feel a need to bite into her neck to get at her precious blood, but I resist the urge. I can hear her heart skip a beat when I do just the right thing, which excites me all the more. I move my mouth away from her veins to subdue the temptation. Our hands roam each other's bodies, careful not to go into the forbidden zones.

I know we both want more but hold back. Today has been a great day. There is no reason to push. Half an hour later, we come up for air. We are both a little sweaty and very turned on. We sit for a while lightly caressing each other, enjoying our time together. It is getting late and I realize I have to leave soon.

"It is close to 10. I should be getting you home," Amber sighs without conviction.

"Yep, we have school tomorrow." I run my hand through her hair to feel it's softness against my palm.

She tilts her head back a little and closes her eyes as I play with her hair. I know I'm just prolonging the inevitable. I kiss her once more and then get up, pulling her to me. We walk out to her car and get in. On the short ride to my house, we talk.

"Do you live with your mom?" Amber wonders.

There is no good way to say this. "Umm...my mom died when I was thirteen. She didn't have any relatives so I was put in the foster system. I live with foster parents," I admit hoping this does not change anything.

Amber looks at me as if she is in shock. She pulls into an empty bank parking lot and parks the car. She leans over and hugs me. "I'm so sorry, Duncan. I cannot imagine losing both my parents." She cries tears that I can no longer muster.

I have been too hurt by it all to have tears left for my dead mom. It is sad that I am so jaded. I know I have had a hard life since mom died, but life before was not that great, either. Sure mom and I had a good relationship, but mom went through men like I go through socks. Most of them were bums and we moved all the time. We never had any money. But, I always loved her. I guess I kind of had to. She was my mom.

I hold Amber until she stops crying. I wipe away her tears and kiss her cheeks. I can taste the salty wetness of her sorrow for me. I love that she cares so much. This girl has stolen my heart.

"You must think I'm silly," Amber apologizes, her cheeks flush with embarrassment.

"No I really love that you care. It means a lot to me that you can share my sadness. It makes me like you even more, Amber." I mean every word.

She looks at me with questioning eyes and I wonder what she is thinking. She seems to make some decision within her mysterious girl mind and smiles at me.

"Can you do me a favor?" Amber asks, as she starts driving to my house again.

"Sure, what you need?"

"When you see that new guy can you tell him he's got a new girlfriend?"

"I know he will be glad to hear that. Lucky guy...," I smile at my new girlfriend.

To read more pick up a copy of _Savage Summer_ at Amazon.com

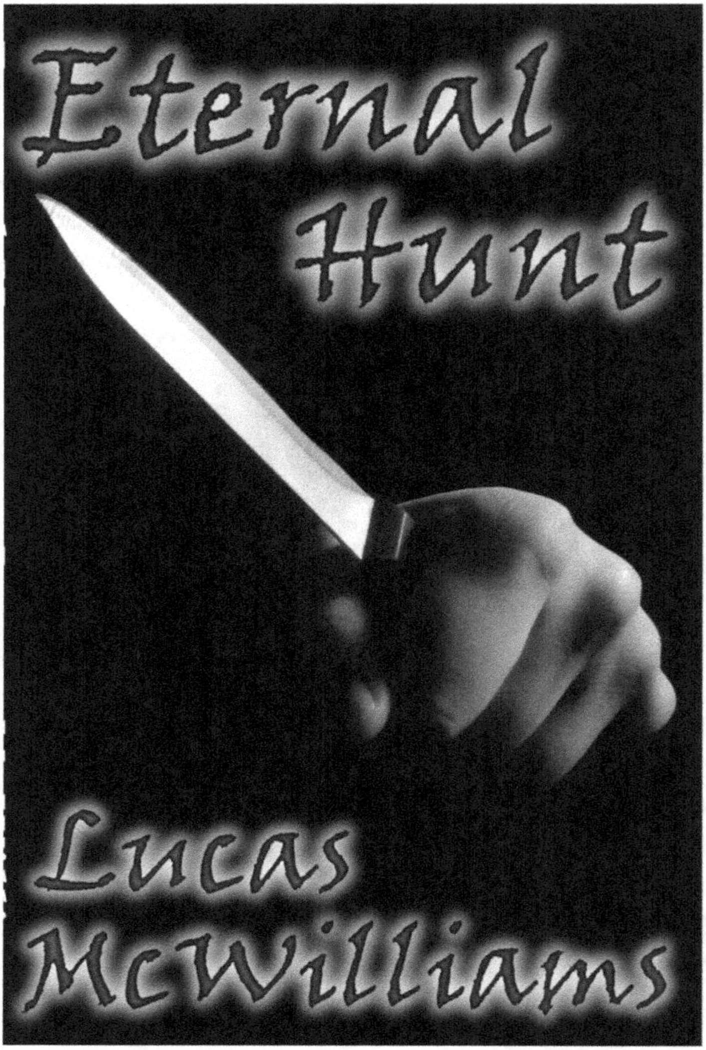
Eternal
Hunt
Lucas
McWilliams

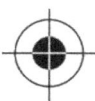

Eternal Hunt: Longstride Chronicles

Set in contemporary Alaska, Canada and New York State, THE ETERNAL HUNT, THE LONGSTRIDE CHRONICLES is an Iroquois Indian legend based supernatural thriller.

While trapped in a month long storm in the Alaskan wilderness Logan's cousin and Indian blood brother, Caleb, becomes a cannibal to survive. Cannibalism opens Caleb's soul up to a vile Indian spirit known as a Wendigo, which possesses him.

After the storm lifts, Logan is the first on the scene to find his friend. All Logan's party finds is death at the hands of the vicious Wendigo that Caleb has become.

Logan barely survives. A near death vision shows Logan he has been chosen by the spirits to take up the knife and hunt the Wendigo.

Logan joins the False Face Society of his tribe, the Seneca Indians of the Iroquois nation. He carves a mask of the Wendigo and upon donning it, gains the Wendigo's powers.

Along the way, Logan is recruited into a secret government organization that monitors supernatural beings. With the combination of their high tech weapons and his Indian spirit powers, they hope to stop the Wendigo. Logan struggles with his desire to save his blood brother and the knowledge that the Cannibalistic Wendigo Sprit inhabiting his body must be stopped at any cost.

Savage Summer

Vampire
Rock and Roll

Lucas McWilliams

Savage Summer

Set in contemporary Seattle, *SAVAGE SUMMER* is a YA novel that is a supernatural thriller as well as a love story.

Seventeen-year-old Duncan is pretty sure he died recently in the car crash that killed his foster mother. His life really gets complicated when he is thrust into a new foster home, a new high school, falls in love with Amber, the hottest redhead in school, joins her rock band Savage Summer and develops a disturbing thirst for blood.

The band, Savage Summer, gets a gig at a local club, Eros, which turns out to be a haven for vampires. Duncan is forced to protect his new girlfriend Amber and the rest of the band from hungry bloodsuckers and the seductive tunes of Zeal, the vampire rock star.

Meanwhile the ruler of the city's vampires, Sapphire, is trying to seduce Duncan. But all Duncan is really interested in is trying to be a normal kid who feels he has finally found a family with Amber and Savage Summer. Duncan struggles with his love for Amber versus the realization she might be safer if he just walked away.

About the Author

Lucas has been writing books for years but just started publishing them. He spends a lot of his time sitting in front of the computer with his oldest daughter, Sophia, writing stories that they come up with together.

Lucas & Sophia live with their family on a hilltop close to the Kentucky River Palisades. Their loving family includes Lucas' wife, the local librarian, two wonderfully silly younger daughters, their cat Kiki and dogs Peanut and Ginger.

You can contact them at
FaceBook
www.Wielders.us
www.LucasMcWilliams.com

Chapter Books by father-daughter team Lucas and Sophia McWilliams

Wielders #1 The Journey Begins
Wielders #2 First Battle
Wielders #3 The Hunter
Wielders #4 Silver Town Championship
Wielders #5 Lost Friend
Wielders #6 Secretes in the Dark
Wielders #7 Water Temple
Wielders #8 Returning Home
Wielders # 9 Resistance
Wielders #10 Journey
And look for more coming out soon!

PLEASE WRITE A REVIEW!
A review is the best way
you can help the author.
Please take a second to go
back to where you
downloaded or bought this
book and write a review.

Thank you so much for
your help in spreading the
word about our book!
Lucas & Sophia